Someone to Love

As Zoe entered the Duke's bedroom he looked round in surprise.

She flung herself against him, crying as she did so:

"Save . . . me . . . save . . . me!"

Her voice was almost incoherent with breathlessness and fear.

The Duke acted instantly.

He drew Zoe quickly along the corridor to a boudoir which connected with her own bedroom.

"Go inside," he said quietly, "and do not open the door until I come back to you."

"You . . . will . . . hide . . . me?" Zoe asked.

"No one will take you away from me," the Duke said firmly.

A Camfield Novel ~~of Lo~~ve
by Barbara ~~Cartland~~

"Barbara Cartla~~n~~ . . . by their intelligence, good . . .

— ~~R~~OMANTIC TIMES

"Who could give bet~~ter~~ . . . how to keep your romance going strong than the w~~orld's~~ most famous romance novelist, Barbara Cartland?"

— THE STAR

Camfield Place,
Hatfield
Hertfordshire,
England

Dearest Reader,

Camfield Novels of Love mark a very exciting era of my books with Jove. They have already published nearly two hundred of my titles since they became my first publisher in America, and now all my original paperback romances in the future will be published exclusively by them.

As you already know, Camfield Place in Hertfordshire is my home, which originally existed in 1275, but was rebuilt in 1867 by the grandfather of Beatrix Potter.

It was here in this lovely house, with the best view in the county, that she wrote *The Tale of Peter Rabbit*. Mr. McGregor's garden is exactly as she described it. The door in the wall that the fat little rabbit could not squeeze underneath and the goldfish pool where the white cat sat twitching its tail are still there.

I had Camfield Place blessed when I came here in 1950 and was so happy with my husband until he died, and now with my children and grandchildren, that I know the atmosphere is filled with love and we have all been very lucky.

It is easy here to write of love and I know you will enjoy the Camfield Novels of Love. Their plots are definitely exciting and the covers very romantic. They come to you, like all my books, with love.

Bless you,

CAMFIELD NOVELS OF LOVE
by Barbara Cartland

THE POOR GOVERNESS
WINGED VICTORY
LUCKY IN LOVE
LOVE AND THE MARQUIS
A MIRACLE IN MUSIC
LIGHT OF THE GODS
BRIDE TO A BRIGAND
LOVE COMES WEST
A WITCH'S SPELL
SECRETS
THE STORMS OF LOVE
MOONLIGHT ON THE
  SPHINX
WHITE LILAC
REVENGE OF THE HEART
THE ISLAND OF LOVE
THERESA AND A TIGER
LOVE IS HEAVEN
MIRACLE FOR A MADONNA
A VERY UNUSUAL WIFE
THE PERIL AND THE
  PRINCE
ALONE AND AFRAID
TEMPTATION OF A
  TEACHER
ROYAL PUNISHMENT
THE DEVILISH DECEPTION
PARADISE FOUND
LOVE IS A GAMBLE
A VICTORY FOR LOVE
LOOK WITH LOVE
NEVER FORGET LOVE
HELGA IN HIDING
SAFE AT LAST
HAUNTED
CROWNED WITH LOVE
ESCAPE
THE DEVIL DEFEATED
THE SECRET OF THE
  MOSQUE
A DREAM IN SPAIN
THE LOVE TRAP
LISTEN TO LOVE
THE GOLDEN CAGE
LOVE CASTS OUT FEAR
A WORLD OF LOVE
DANCING ON A RAINBOW
LOVE JOINS THE CLANS
AN ANGEL RUNS AWAY
FORCED TO MARRY
BEWILDERED IN BERLIN

WANTED—A WEDDING
  RING
THE EARL ESCAPES
STARLIGHT OVER TUNIS
THE LOVE PUZZLE
LOVE AND KISSES
SAPPHIRES IN SIAM
A CARETAKER OF LOVE
SECRETS OF THE HEART
RIDING IN THE SKY
LOVERS IN LISBON
LOVE IS INVINCIBLE
THE GODDESS OF LOVE
AN ADVENTURE OF LOVE
THE HERB FOR HAPPINESS
ONLY A DREAM
SAVED BY LOVE
LITTLE TONGUES OF FIRE
A CHIEFTAIN FINDS LOVE
A LOVELY LIAR
THE PERFUME OF THE
  GODS
A KNIGHT IN PARIS
REVENGE IS SWEET
THE PASSIONATE PRINCESS
SOLITA AND THE SPIES
THE PERFECT PEARL
LOVE IS A MAZE
A CIRCUS FOR LOVE
THE TEMPLE OF LOVE
THE BARGAIN BRIDE
THE HAUNTED HEART
REAL LOVE OR FAKE
KISS FROM A STRANGER
A VERY SPECIAL LOVE
THE NECKLACE OF LOVE
A REVOLUTION OF LOVE
THE MARQUIS WINS
LOVE IS THE KEY
LOVE AT FIRST SIGHT
THE TAMING OF A TIGRESS
PARADISE IN PENANG
THE EARL RINGS A BELLE
THE QUEEN SAVES THE
  KING
NO DISGUISE FOR LOVE
LOVE LIFTS THE CURSE
BEAUTY OR BRAINS?
TOO PRECIOUS TO LOSE
HIDING
A TANGLED WEB

JUST FATE
A MIRACLE IN MEXICO
WARNED BY A GHOST
TWO HEARTS IN HUNGARY
A THEATER OF LOVE
A DYNASTY OF LOVE
MAGIC FROM THE HEART
THE WINDMILL OF LOVE
LOVE STRIKES A DEVIL
LOVE AND WAR
SEEK THE STARS
A CORONATION OF LOVE
A WISH COMES TRUE
LOVED FOR HIMSELF
A KISS IN ROME
HIDDEN BY LOVE
BORN OF LOVE
WALKING TO
  WONDERLAND
TERROR FROM THE
  THRONE
THE CAVE OF LOVE
THE PEAKS OF ECSTASY
LUCKY LOGAN FINDS LOVE
THE ANGEL AND THE
  RAKE
THE QUEEN OF HEARTS
THE WICKED WIDOW
TO SCOTLAND AND LOVE
LOVE AT THE RITZ
THE DANGEROUS
  MARRIAGE
GOOD OR BAD?
THIS IS LOVE
RUNNING AWAY TO LOVE
LOOK WITH THE HEART
SAFE IN PARADISE
THE DUKE FINDS LOVE
THE WONDERFUL DREAM
A ROYAL REBUKE
THE DARE-DEVIL DUKE
NEVER LOSE LOVE
THE SPIRIT OF LOVE
THE EYES OF LOVE
SAVED BY A SAINT
THE INCOMPARABLE
THE INNOCENT IMPOSTOR
THE LOVELESS MARRIAGE
A MAGICAL MOMENT
THE PATIENT BRIDEGROOM
THE PROTECTION OF LOVE
RUNNING FROM RUSSIA

A NEW CAMFIELD NOVEL OF LOVE BY

Barbara Cartland

Someone to Love

JOVE BOOKS, NEW YORK

SOMEONE TO LOVE

A Jove Book/published by arrangement with the author

PRINTING HISTORY
Jove edition/August 1995

ISBN: 0-515-11686-6

A JOVE BOOK®
Jove Books are published by The Berkley Publishing Group,
200 Madison Avenue, New York, New York 10016.
JOVE and the "J" design are trademarks
belonging to Jove Publications, Inc.

PRINTED IN THE UNITED STATES OF AMERICA

10 9 8 7 6 5 4 3 2 1

Author's Note

FOR the best part of a century, the *Great Game*, which was an extraordinarily unusual and brilliantly conceived Secret Service, played a large part in the Government of India.

Many British regular soldiers, political officers who were good at languages, traders, and quite a number of amateurs and travellers took part.

The aim was to protect India with its limitless markets and fabulous wealth from the greed of the Russians.

Those who worked in the *Great Game* gathered political and other intelligence, discovered possible invasion routes, and detected Spies who were beginning to rise up in every part of India.

It was Catherine the Great's troops who first started to fight their way South through the Caucasus towards Persia.

British fears intensified when Napoleon in 1807

proposed to Tsar Alexander that they should invade the enticing East together.

In fact, Napoleon with his great ambitions told Alexander they might, if they combined their armies, conquer the whole world between them.

As I have said in this novel, when the *Great Game* first began, the frontiers of British India and Russia were over two thousand miles apart.

In the end in London and St. Petersburg in 1907 they reached an understanding and by then this gap had shrunk in places to less than twenty miles.

Before this it was no secret to the British that the Russian Officers in central Asia drank toasts and thought of little except the invasion of India.

For a young man, the *Great Game* was an exciting drama in which he had always dreamt of taking part.

It was a chance to escape from the monotony of Garrison life in the hot, sweltering plains, and although they took their lives in their hands, there was always a chance of promotion and glory.

Some died; some went out on a mission and never returned.

There was still the excitement, the adventure, the thrill, and, of course, the secrecy which was irresistible.

Someone
to Love

chapter one

1874

THE Duke of Stalbridge lay back in bed with a sigh of relief.

Everything had gone as well as he had hoped, and he told himself he was a very lucky man.

For the first time in his life the Duke had admitted he was in love.

With just a certain amount of hesitation on his part, he had proposed marriage.

He was not surprised that Lady Lois Minford had accepted him eagerly.

He had been pursued by women ever since he had left Eton.

Even his years in the Army had been colourful for the number of *affaires de coeur* in which he had indulged.

It was not really surprising, considering he was without dispute one of the most handsome men in London.

His title was an old one, and after he inherited from his Father he was exceedingly rich.

The Duke had learned very early in life to be fastidious and discriminating in all personal matters.

He was also, although only those close to him realised it, extremely intelligent.

This had qualified him, although it was a complete secret, to play a part when he was soldiering in India in the *Great Game*.

This was the most successful and the most exciting Secret Service ever organised by the British.

It was, of course, impossible for the Duke, after he came into the title, to stay in the *Great Game* or even in the Army.

He had had to come back to look after his huge Estate, and inevitably to be pursued by every ambitious Mother with a marriageable daughter.

He had been amused by the commotion he caused.

As he said to one of his men friends: "Women are paraded in front of me like horses at a Spring sale."

He had, however, no intention of marrying until he fell in love.

When it eventually happened, it quite surprised him!

There was no doubt, however, that Lady Lois Minford was exceptionally lovely.

As the daughter of the Marquess and Marchioness of Minfordbury, she belonged to a family that equalled the Duke's.

It, too, was one of the oldest in British history.

When the Duke finally proposed marriage, he knew that his family would be overjoyed.

They must naturally be the first to be informed of his decision.

His Aunts, Cousins, and what Grandparents remained had almost gone on their knees begging him when he reached his twenty-sixth birthday to take a wife.

"You *must* have a son, Ivor," they all repeated over and over again until the Duke was tired of hearing it.

They pointed out that the heir presumptive to the Dukedom, until he had a son, was an elderly Cousin.

He had never married and was noted as being a recluse.

"Can you imagine what Frederick would do to the Estate?" they asked. "And to your horses at Newmarket, your house in London, your collection of Orchids?"

The last warning amused the Duke.

He knew that the majority of his relatives did not understand this particular interest which he had taken up when he was serving in India.

He had gone to Nepal and was thrilled by the magnificent and varied Orchids he saw on the foot-hills of the Himalayas.

During the last year of his service he had gone further.

He had entered Tibet and brought back even more plants to add to those he had already.

In his absence two new greenhouses had been erected on his instructions at Stalbridge Hall.

Already one of them was full and he had almost completed filling the other.

It seemed a strange interest for a young man, especially for the Duke, whom no-one could accuse of being anything but entirely masculine.

He was an outstanding horseman and extremely athletic.

He kept himself fit and slim so that he always appeared to be on top of his form.

He was ready to challenge anyone, not only at

games, but at any activity which required use of the brain.

There had been a great deal to be done at the Hall when he returned from India.

His Mother had died three years before his Father.

The house had been allowed to get rather shabby, repairs had been neglected, and many of the servants were too old for their jobs.

When the Duke inherited, he was determined that everything about the place should be perfect.

He had learned a great deal from his travels.

He had seen how other people lived, whether they were Kings, Viceroys, Sheiks, Maharajas, or Aristocrats in other countries.

He knew exactly what he wanted for generations.

In the last century the house had been practically rebuilt by the Adam brothers.

They had made it a most perfect example of finest Palladian in the country.

Lying now in the Master Suite, the Duke was in a four-poster bed which had been used by his ancestors for three hundred years.

The posts and the canopy had been regilded, and the heavy velvet curtains replaced.

The Stalbridge coat-of-arms was re-embroidered at the back of the bed.

It all looked magnificent.

The same applied to the rest of the room.

The carpets had been replaced, as had the window-curtains, and the furniture repaired.

The Duke had been wise and knowledgeable enough to know which pieces in the Hall were genuine.

Some had been replaced over the years by imitations or inferior pieces.

It gave him a great deal of pleasure to sort out and keep only what was the best.

This was why a number of pictures in the Picture Gallery had been removed.

They were hung in upstairs rooms and replaced by others which had not been properly appreciated or in some cases actually sold.

It was surprising how many people had in their possession pictures and *objets d'art* which had once belonged to Stalbridge Hall.

They were quite prepared to sell them back to the present occupier—at a profit.

Lying in bed, the Duke thought it was very satisfactory that Lois had admired effusively everything she had seen.

"Why did you not tell me," she said in her soft, seductive voice, "that you lived, not in a house, but a Palace?"

"I am glad you should think so," the Duke answered.

He knew she would look very beautiful at the end of the great dining-table, wearing the Stalbridge jewels.

These were famous.

It had been said that at Queen Victoria's private collection could be rivalled by that owned by the Duke of Stalbridge.

He knew that Lois would look breathtaking in the diamond tiara.

The sapphire collection would undoubtedly enhance the whiteness of her skin.

He was not so sure about the ruby set.

He had always thought rubies should be worn only by brunettes.

He remembered a very attractive brunette he had

known in Paris who had persuaded him to give her a necklace of rubies.

She thanked him by wearing it that night when he took her to bed.

She laughed when he complained that it scratched his chin.

Now he told himself there were so many things he would want to give Lois.

He was quite certain she would thank him very graciously.

She had been excessively grateful for the small gifts he had given her while they were getting to know each other.

Flowers, scent, chocolates—these were by convention the only presents an unmarried girl was allowed to accept.

It had all happened very quickly.

The Duke was not so foolish as not to realise that the Marquess of Minfordbury was eager to have a rich son-in-law.

His houses cost a considerable sum to keep up.

He was an extravagant man by nature.

His horses were not successful on the race-course.

He, however, undoubtedly had a winner in his daughter, Lois.

He was determined to find the right husband for her.

There was, in fact, no competition where the Duke was concerned.

They had met by chance at a Ball given a month ago.

After the Duke had danced three times with Lois, the Marquess was sure he was on the way to the winning-post.

Wherever the Duke went the following week, Lady

Lois "happened" to be there.

He also received from the Marquess invitations to Dinner and one to spend a weekend at the Minfordbury house in the country.

As it happened, he had to refuse this because of another commitment, but he had driven down for Luncheon on the Sunday.

He had been impressed both by the antiquity of the Marquess's house and by the Marchioness, who he thought was charming.

He had always thought that if he did marry, it was important that he should like his in-laws.

That they would like him was, of course, a foregone conclusion.

Then, as the days passed, he found himself dancing with Lois almost every evening, talking with her at Luncheon, even meeting her apparently by chance in Rotten Row when he rode before Breakfast.

He told himself he was in love.

After the sophisticated and somewhat exotic women with whom he had flirted these past years, he found Lois intriguing.

He was fascinated by her innocence and what he thought was her shyness.

She made no advances towards him.

She was, he had noticed, always hesitant before she agreed to do anything of which she thought her Father and Mother might disapprove.

This, he told himself, was what he wanted in his wife.

When he finally proposed, she had not lifted her lips to his as any other woman would have done.

Instead, she hid her face against his shoulder.

"Are you ... quite ... certain," she asked, "that

since I am so . . . young you will not . . . find me . . . dull?"

"I adore you because you are young," the Duke said, "and it will be very exciting for me to teach you about love."

He thought as he spoke he had never wanted a wife who, like so many women he knew, "made the running."

He had grown very much more authoritative as he got older.

He wanted to rule not only his house and his Estate, but also his wife.

The women who had offered him their favours almost before he knew their names had planned exactly how they would captivate him, then utilised every trick in the book to do so.

Lois, instead of looking knowingly into his eyes, looked away.

She appeared to blush when he complimented her and he found it was all new and definitely exciting.

"We will have a long Honeymoon," he told himself, "and when we return she will no longer be shy."

He was sure that teaching her to take her place as a Duchess would give her confidence.

She would rely on him for support and guidance.

'That is what I want,' he thought.

He told himself he must be very gentle with someone so young and innocent so that he did not frighten her.

He realised as he lay in bed that he had not, as he normally did, gone straight to sleep.

"I suppose it is because I am excited at what is happening this weekend," he told himself.

He had come down from London to Stalbridge Hall that afternoon.

He had travelled in his private carriage attached to the train which stopped, if requested, at the halt at Stalbridge.

He had brought with him the Marquess and Marchioness of Minfordbury, and, of course, the lovely Lois, also his friend Charles Barnell.

Lord Barnell, as he now was, had been at Eton with the Duke.

They had gone on to Oxford together before the Duke had joined his Regiment.

Charles was his greatest friend and he amused the Duke more than any other man he had ever met.

They were complete opposites in character.

While the Duke was so clever and determined in anything he undertook, Charles just enjoyed himself.

His Father was a Peer who had done the same, and managed to run through his entire fortune in the process.

He had left his only son nothing but his title and his debts.

Charles's Father had in fact been a genius at losing a fortune at cards, and inevitably backing the wrong horse in every race.

Yet he managed to laugh at his own stupidity.

He died when he was seventy-six, laughing because he had just been told he had put two women "in the family way."

His mountain of debts would have made everyone except Charles utterly despondent.

Instead, quite openly and making no pretence about it, he begged from his Father's friends and his own to pay them off.

Because they liked Charles, and he amused them, nearly everyone had contributed.

Once he had his head above water, Charles was

quite content to live unashamedly off his friends.

The extraordinary thing was that while everyone knew that Charles was a sponger and the last man any woman would want her daughter to marry, he was invariably invited to every party.

This was because just by being there, Charles could make every party a success.

He kept the guests laughing and seemed to raise the tempo the moment he entered a room.

The Duke was only too ready to share with Charles almost everything he possessed.

His horses in the country were at his disposal as well as his house in Grosvenor Square.

The Mews behind it provided Charles with a Chaise to drive or a horse to ride whenever he wanted.

"You surely do not want me to come down with you the night before the majority of your party arrives," Charles had said when the Duke told him they were going to the country on Thursday.

"Of course I want you," the Duke answered. "I will find Minfordbury heavy on the hand if you are not there to make us laugh. Also, I want you to help me plan the seating for the big party on Saturday night."

"Is that when you are going to announce your engagement?" Charles asked.

"I thought," the Duke said, "I would have all my relations in the house or staying with neighbours. They will meet Lois at dinner on Friday evening or at the Point-to-Point on Saturday morning. The most important moment will be Saturday evening."

"Go on," Charles prompted, "I am most impressed."

"We will have a large dinner-party," the Duke said, "at which I will announce publicly that Lois and I are to be married, and afterwards there will be dancing in the Ball-room."

"It sounds delightful," Charles exclaimed.

"It is going to take a lot of organising," the Duke said. "The Point-to-Point is easy because it takes place every year. But I expect you will want to ride in it, and there are several horses you can choose from."

"Of course I want the winner," Charles remarked.

"Then you had better not drink too much on Friday evening," the Duke replied. "You threw the race away last year after the third, or was it the fourth, glass of brandy."

Charles had merely laughed.

"You had better double the prize this year, then I will really try hard for it."

The Duke then told Charles that he had asked his closest relatives to stay on Friday and Saturday night.

This included his Grandmother on his Father's side, to whom he was devoted, also several Aunts and Uncles who had always loved him since he was a small boy, and a number of his favourite Cousins.

Charles knew them all.

Then he added:

"Are most of them going to be arriving on Friday?"

"My Grandmother and my Aunt Margaret, whom of course you know, will be there on Thursday with us."

Charles had nodded.

The Duke knew that whether or not Charles would be delighted to see them, they would be delighted to see him.

He had a way with older people, and his Grandmother always asked:

"How is that charming friend of yours, Charles Barnell? He is so amusing."

Because the train was late, she and the Duke's Aunt were waiting at the Hall when he and his party arrived.

His Grandmother was seventy, but she still carried herself with a dignity which he admired.

He knew she had always been very anxious as to whom he would marry.

"You cannot expect me, Grandmother," the Duke had said to her several times, "to find someone as beautiful as you sitting outside the front door."

The Dowager had appreciated the compliment.

She had in fact been a great beauty and extremely happy with her husband.

Although she too had pressed the Duke to marry, she worried in case he married the wrong girl.

She thought many of the *débutantes* of today were not likely to make as good wives as those of her generation.

It was what all elderly people thought.

Though the Dowager Duchess had enough sense of humour to laugh at herself, at the same time, her grandson was very precious to her.

She prayed fervently that when he did marry he would be very happy.

Dinner had certainly passed off successfully, and that was entirely due to Charles.

He had made them laugh and they had most discreetly not talked about the reason they were there and what was going to happen on Saturday night.

Only when they were going up to bed did the Duke find quite by accident that he and Lois were left alone in the Drawing-Room.

The others were moving slowly across the hall.

"I have not had a chance to talk to you," the Duke

12

said in a low voice, "or to tell you how very beautiful you look."

Her eyelids fluttered against her cheeks in a way he thought extremely attractive.

"I want . . . you to think . . . so," she said in a murmur.

The Duke put his arm around her and bent his head towards her lips.

But she moved so that instead he kissed her cheek.

"Tomorrow," he said gently, "I have so much to show you, and then perhaps we will be alone."

"I would . . . like that," she whispered. "Now I . . . had better . . . go."

She ran after her Father and Mother as if she were afraid they would be angry with her.

The Duke thought that no-one could be more entrancing.

"We will make it a very short time before we are married," he told himself, "just long enough for her to get her trousseau. Then we can be alone."

He had felt a thrill run through him at the idea.

Still not having fallen asleep, he suddenly thought of something romantic that he could give her at this very moment.

When he had come up to bed, his Valet had said to him:

"I was asked to tell Your Grace that the Orchid you brought from Tibet has come into bloom."

The Duke was delighted.

This, he thought, was another piece of luck that he had not expected.

The Orchid he had bought in Tibet was called *Chusua Donii* and would grow only, they told him, at a very high altitude.

He had, however, brought the plant back with him.

He was determined to try to see if he could get it to flower at Stalbridge.

When he had looked at it two weeks ago, it was alive and seemed not particularly disturbed at being transplanted.

It was obviously an omen that his marriage would be as perfect and beautiful as the *Chusua Donii* flower itself.

It was white, the colour of purity, and that, of course, was Lois herself.

On an impulse he got up and put on a long, dark robe which his Valet had left lying over a chair.

He brushed his hair back from his forehead before he walked to the door.

It was now after one o'clock and the house was still and quiet.

He deliberately did not go down the main staircase which led to the hall.

The Night-Footman would be on duty there.

The man would probably be asleep, but at this particular moment the Duke had no wish to talk to anyone.

Instead, he let himself out by the garden-door.

He walked across the lawn in the moonlight in the direction of the greenhouses.

Those housing his precious Orchids had been built at the back of the shrubbery.

They were not connected in any way to the old greenhouses in which an enormous amount of flowers were raised for the rooms at the Hall and were also taken up every week to London when the Duke was in residence there.

With the flowers went up the vegetables, the butter, the cream, and the eggs, also chickens, hams, ducks, and lambs when in season from the Home Farm.

It was something which required a lot of organisation.

Here again the Duke expected perfection and was seldom disappointed.

The air was cool outside; there was no wind.

The stars were like diamonds in the sky, and a young moon was climbing up the Heavens.

Its silver beams shone on the lake and lighted the garden, making the shadows beneath the trees magical and mysterious.

When the Duke walked in his garden at night, he felt he entered another world from the one in which he ordinarily lived.

He could not explain it fully even to himself.

Somehow the fairy stories his Mother had read to him when he was a child, and the strange legends he had found in different parts of the world, all seemed to knit together in the garden of his home.

He almost felt as if the trees spoke to him.

The cascade splashing down the rock-garden told him secrets which other people did not know.

It was something he had never spoken of to his friends, not even to Charles.

They would have laughed at him, accusing him of just being imaginative.

He thought one day he would talk about it to the woman he loved, and she would understand.

He passed on through the shrubbery and came to where the greenhouses were concealed behind it.

It was a perfect place because it was near enough for the Duke to reach them easily whenever he wished.

At the same time, they did not appear obtrusive to anyone walking in the Garden.

As the Duke opened the door, he felt the special

excitement which was always there as he did so.

Each plant was different from anything else he possessed, and each was a part of his life.

He had travelled to many places, not only because he wanted to see the world, but because he wanted to understand the other people living in it.

Each journey widened and developed his knowledge of the human race.

He had brought back many souvenirs, carvings from Africa, pearls from the Gulf, jewels from India, and some exquisite Icons from Russia.

Above all, he had brought, and this to him was the most important, Orchids from every country which grew them.

With every new addition to his collection he learned more about what to him was the most beautiful flower in existence.

Now for the moment he did not light a lantern.

These were always kept in the greenhouses so that he could go there at any time of the day or night.

He looked at the moonlight coming through the glass and it showed him the flowers he knew so well.

There was a bright pink *Dendrobium*, the yellow of the *Cymbidium*, the purple of *Laeliocattleya*, and, of course, the white of *Odontonia*.

He passed them one after another, and sometimes he put out his hand just to touch a petal very, very gently.

He thought it was as soft as Lois's cheek had been.

"She will be thrilled," he told himself, "when I show her these Orchids tomorrow."

He passed into the second greenhouse, and now he had eyes only for the *Chusua Donii* for which he had come.

He had put it at the far end, standing by itself.

It was kept cool between blocks of ice from the Ice House in the lake.

In the moonlight he could see it quite clearly, and when he did so he felt his heart leap.

It was in blossom.

There was the white breaking through, and just one flower was almost in full bloom.

This was a triumph, a triumph which he knew would be a surprise to his rival enthusiasts.

They had all told him it was quite impossible to expect a plant from the heights of Tibet to flourish in England.

The Duke picked up the plant to hold in his hand and to look at it more closely than he had before.

He would dedicate it to Lois.

What could be more exciting than for her to wake up tomorrow morning and find it in her room?

Just for a moment he hesitated in case it should in any way hurt the plant.

Then he told himself he would take it back immediately after breakfast.

At least she would have the thrill of knowing that he laid at her feet something which he cherished perhaps more than anything else he possessed.

"I am sure she will understand," he told himself.

Very gently, holding the plant with both hands, he moved out of the greenhouse, shutting the door carefully behind him.

Then, as he walked across the lawn, he felt like a Knight at King Arthur's Court holding the Holy Grail.

He had found the flower after a tremendous search, and now it was his and no-one should take it from him.

He wanted to say a prayer of gratitude.

In fact, it was in his mind as he reached the door

through which he had left the house.

He went up to the first floor.

From there he still had a long walk to the West Wing, where his guests were staying.

There were only a few rooms near his own, which were State Rooms kept mostly for Royalty.

They were not in use except very occasionally.

Some would, of course, be used when the house was full on Saturday night; the Duke's Grandmother was in one already.

The Marquess and Marchioness were in the West Wing in the most important rooms at the far end, and their daughter was not very far from them.

The Duke had previously worked out a room-plan with his Secretary.

He knew exactly where Lady Lois's room was situated.

On returning to the house he had changed into suede bedroom slippers embroidered with his crest, and moving soundlessly, he reached her door.

He wondered whether he should lay the Orchid outside it.

Then he told himself the maid who called Lady Lois might be stupid enough to think it was of no importance and not take it in.

He was quite certain that Lois would be asleep by now.

The bedroom was very large, and if he opened the door very quietly, she would not hear him.

He had learned when he was in the *Great Game* how to move without making a sound.

This had undoubtedly saved his life on two or three occasions, when to have been discovered would have meant certain death.

Holding the Orchid with his left hand, the Duke

turned the handle of the door very slowly.

It did not make any sound, and the door opened.

It was then that he heard someone laughing, and he stiffened.

In fact, it was as if he were turned to stone.

The laugh he had heard was made by a man.

It was the Duke's training which enabled him to keep completely and absolutely still.

Then he heard Lois's soft little voice say something which he could not quite hear.

Again there was the laugh which he recognised to be Charles's, and the Duke heard him say quite clearly:

"More and more do I find you utterly entrancing! Kiss me again, Darling, in case this is the last time we can be together."

"I cannot bear it," Lois replied. "You must come to me again tomorrow night, however dangerous it may be."

"How can I refuse you?" Charles asked.

Then the Duke was aware Charles was kissing Lois passionately as they lay in bed together.

He had only to take a few steps forward, and as one candle was lit on the far side of the bed he would be able to see them quite clearly.

Just for a moment he felt impelled to confront them, to tell them what he thought of them.

Then he knew it would be a mistake.

Instead, he gently pulled the door to, turning the handle slowly until it was closed completely.

He walked back the way he had come, moving silently across the soft carpet until he reached his own room and changed his shoes.

Then he went down the side staircase he had used before.

He opened the door into the Garden and went back to the greenhouse.

He put the Orchid back in its place between the ice blocks.

He felt as if the whole world had turned into disarray in front of him.

How was it possible that Lois, the only woman whom he had ever wanted to marry and who he believed would make a perfect wife, was in bed with his friend, Charles?

It seemed to the Duke incredible that it had actually happened.

Now, with his astute brain, he began to see what he had not noticed before.

It was Charles, he guessed, who had told Lois exactly how she could attract him by seeming shy and innocent.

Now he thought about it, Minfordbury had been one of those who had subscribed generously towards the payment of Charles's Father's debts.

Charles, therefore, owed him something.

How could he pay him back better than by helping to get Lois married to the richest Duke in the country?

The Duke found it all passing through his mind.

He could remember only too clearly now that every time he had visited Lois at her house, Charles had been there.

It must have been Charles, too, who had managed to arrange that Lois was at every Party he attended.

He always found her sitting on one side of him at Dinner.

The Duke found that, strangely enough, he was not resenting the part that Charles had played in all this manoeuvering, or even the fact that it was he who was already Lois's lover.

He was generous enough to realise that Charles, as his friend, was not trying to hurt him.

He was merely helping to get him married to produce an heir as his family had long thought was his duty.

What Charles had done was to encourage the first interest he had shown in Lois.

He had helped to bait the trap that the Marquess quickly laid for him.

'A trap!' the Duke thought bitterly.

He would be marrying a woman who was not the innocent virgin he had expected her to be.

She already had a lover in Charles, and for all he knew, many other men before him.

He wanted perfection.

He wanted his wife to be different from all the other women he had known.

He had not contemplated for a moment that she would be anything but pure and untouched.

It was what he had supposed all young *débutantes* to be.

It had never even crossed his mind that any of them would be anything else, above all the one he had chosen for himself.

He knew now he had been caught in a trap from which he had to escape, not only for his own self-respect, but for any hope of happiness he might find in marriage.

The Duke was on the whole a good-tempered man.

But when he was angry or really disturbed by something another person had done, he was very formidable.

In cases involving cruelty either to animals or to children he was completely ruthless.

He punished mercilessly those who he knew had committed such a crime.

Now, as his anger rose again, he became, as always, at the same time very calm.

His brain began to work like a machine, swiftly and with a determination that was unappeasable.

He wanted now not only to tell Lois he had no use for her but also to make her suffer.

He felt the same about those members of his family who had been so insistent that he must marry.

Why could they not have left him alone?

Instead, they had brought pressure to bear so that he was never free of it.

He could see all too easily now how they were always pleading with him, the parents who wanted him as a son-in-law tempting him, and contriving that he had little chance to escape.

Now, by the grace of God, he had been caught just in time to save him from announcing his engagement to a woman who had deceived and lied to him even before she was his wife.

He felt his anger surging within him.

At the same time, quietly, he started to work out what he could do.

It was not going to be easy, but this was a problem to which somehow he had to find an answer.

chapter two

THE Duke, having had hardly any sleep, rose early and pulled back the curtains.

He looked out and saw it was a sunny morning.

He thought the best thing he could do was to go riding.

All through the night and still ringing in his ears was the question of how he should handle his dilemma.

How could he extract himself from the situation with the least fuss?

What he disliked more than anything else were accusations, recriminations, and, most of all, tears.

He had suffered quite a lot in this respect from the women he had left.

This, however, was a very different proposition.

He could hardly go to the Marquess and say that his daughter was behaving in an improper manner behind his back.

Obviously the Marquess would want to know how he knew.

The Duke realised he would have some difficulty in explaining why he was wandering about in the West Wing in the early hours of the morning.

He could not bear anyone to know that he was romantic enough to wish to put his precious Orchid in Lois's bedroom.

He dressed himself without ringing for his Valet and walked to the Stables.

The Chief Groom was surprised to see him so early, and hurried to saddle his favourite Stallion.

When the Duke rode away, the Chief Groom looked after him anxiously.

He knew by the hardness of his eyes and the stiffness of his lips that something was wrong.

The Duke rode to the flat land and galloped his horse until it was sweating.

Then, as they calmed down to a slower pace, he began to think again what he should do.

It suddenly occurred to him there was one way he could extricate himself with dignity from the mess he was in.

That was by producing someone else to take Lois's place.

When all his relatives were waiting on Saturday night after Dinner for him to announce that he intended to be married, he could hardly say he had changed his mind.

That would cause a sensation as explosive as dropping a bomb on the Dining-Room table.

They had come to be told the joyful news that he was to take a wife.

Most of them were not in the London circle and did not suspect already who his fiancée was.

Therefore, to extricate himself he had to produce a woman whom they would accept as the Duchess of Stalbridge.

The more he thought over this idea, the more it appealed to him.

It would mean that nothing need be said today which would give Lois the slightest hint that he had discovered she was deceiving him.

There would be the Point-to-Point on Saturday morning.

He had already arranged a demonstration of jumping in the afternoon.

That would amuse the large crowd who always came to Stalbridge Hall on these occasions.

Nothing would be said that would give anyone the slightest suspicion that he and Lois were not in perfect harmony.

That was how they had appeared to be when they arrived from London last night.

Then at the very last moment he would produce someone else whom he would introduce as his future wife.

He was quite certain that those of his relations who thought they were in the know would be too stunned to say anything.

He had, as he had told Charles, arranged for there to be dancing in the Ball-Room.

That would take place immediately Dinner was over.

He could almost see it happening in front of his eyes.

He knew, as in everything he did, he would work out every detail and there would be no possibility of anything going wrong.

The difficulty was, of course, to find someone he

could introduce in Lois's place.

What he really needed was an actress.

But it would be impossible to get one at such short notice.

Even if he did, it would be hard to dispose of her swiftly, before his relatives could cross-examine her to find out her background.

"What can I do? What can I do?" It was the question that had been hammering in his ears all night.

What he minded more than anything else was that he personally had been deceived.

Ever since he had been in the *Great Game* he had prided himself on having a perception which was superior to that of the ordinary man.

Most of the players in the Imperialist Game were professionals, and those whom the Duke knew had taught him a great deal.

They had been chosen for their linguistic and other gifts by the heads of the organisation in the Viceroy's House in Calcutta.

There also were, of course, amateurs like himself who found the challenge irresistible.

Yet, whoever they might be, the Duke was sure they all had that particular power of perception.

It was a gift essential for keeping them alive while they strove to keep the Russians out of India.

What they were doing was exceedingly dangerous, politically sensitive, and a gamble ultimately of life and death.

Yet, if India was to be preserved, the bravery, the intelligence, and the perception of those in the *Great Game* was indispensable.

The Duke had known of this.

He prided himself on having been extremely successful in the tasks he had carried out on behalf of the Powers that be.

He had been especially thanked for what he had been able to do.

How then, having pitted his brains against the most brilliant Oriental Schemers and behind them the Russians, could he have been deceived by a young girl?

He felt humiliated, to say the least, and was determined to have his revenge.

He had always told himself that however difficult a problem seemed, nothing was impossible.

It was therefore not impossible that now, even at this last moment, he could find someone he could introduce in Lois's place as his future wife.

It would not only surprise his relatives but it would teach Lois, he thought bitterly, a lesson she would not forget.

Where, where, could he find a substitute?

By now he was riding slowly under the trees.

The sunshine was coming through them, casting a pattern on the path in front of him.

It was the kind of romantic setting that he had imagined during this past week for Lois.

He wanted to tell her how much the woods had meant to him when he was a small boy, how he had then believed they were inhabited by fairies and goblins.

There were nymphs in the woodland pools where the kingcups grew.

He had thought she would understand because she was little more than a child herself.

But he knew now she was very much a woman, lusting after men as did all the other women he had known.

His fingers tightened on the reins as he thought of

how easily she had deceived him by appearing to be so young and shy.

"Fool, fool, that I am!" he chided himself, and felt his anger surge within him.

Then, almost like a message from Heaven, he thought of the Orphanage.

It came to him that perhaps there he could find what he sought and, if so, it would be a just reward for a good deed.

Last year he had been in Armenia, just south of the Caucasus Mountains.

He had decided to go to the Caucasus because he had heard the Orchids there were very fine.

He also had a friend, whom he had not seen for years, who had invited him to stay.

He must have mentioned in the Club that he was going there, because the next day he was sent for by the Prime Minister.

Benjamin Disraeli, whom the Duke liked enormously, had welcomed him to 10 Downing Street, saying:

"I want your help."

"You know, Prime Minister, if there is anything I can do for you, it will be a privilege."

The Duke meant this most sincerely because he was a tremendous admirer of Mr. Disraeli's.

He knew that his feelings were echoed by the Queen's.

"I heard through the grapevine," the Prime Minister said, "that you are going to Russia."

"There is nothing secret about it," the Duke answered. "I am going simply as myself and not in any other capacity."

He knew the Prime Minister was aware he had been in the *Great Game*.

He had been grateful to him on one occasion for the information he had brought back from an extremely dangerous mission.

"When you have seen your friend," the Prime Minister said after a moment's hesitation, "I wonder if it would be possible for you to suggest quite casually that you would like to stay a night or two with Prince Kaknovski."

The Duke raised his eyebrows.

"I have heard of him," he said, "but I have never met him."

"I expect you have heard the same stories about his private life as I have," the Prime Minister said, "but what really concerns me is to know how deeply involved he is in Russia's determination to eventually conquer India."

There was no need for him to say more.

Both men knew that when the first shadow of Russian ambition appeared in the East, British India and Russia lay about two thousand miles apart.

Yet one by one the fast-riding Cossacks were expanding the Tzar's Empire.

One after another the ancient caravan towns and the khanates fell to the Cossacks.

It was now no secret to the British that the Russians in central Asia thought of little else but the invasion of India.

That was why the *Great Game* had come into play.

"I have heard some very unpleasant rumours about Prince Kaknovski," the Duke said, "but I did not think there was anything else. Those are his personal predictions, and I did not know he was interested in other directions."

"That is exactly what I want you to find out," the Prime Minister said. "You know that as his Guest and an English nobleman, it would be easier for you than for anyone else."

The Duke knew this was true.

The Russians would treat his title with respect as they respected their own.

From what he had heard of the Prince, he behaved in a way which was a cross between a Roman Emperor and a Turkish Sultan.

"I will do my best," he promised.

When, two months later, he reached the Prince's Palace, which was near Yerevan, he was astonished at the magnificence in which he lived.

All the pomp and glory of the Viceroy and the Maharajas with whom he had stayed in India paled beside the extravagance and Regal way of life of the Prince.

A man getting on for forty, his unrestrained debauchery had made him somewhat unpleasant to look at.

At the same time, it would have been a mistake to under-rate his intelligence.

As the Duke talked to him, he realised they were fencing with words.

He also became aware that despite the Prince's addiction to sexual perversions and an endless parade of young women, he was also ambitious politically.

He was only too willing to strike a blow for Russia, not because he loved his country, but because it would glorify him as a man.

The Duke ate the food that he could describe only as superlative.

He drank wine that on the Prince's instruction had been brought all the way from France.

He was offered before he retired to bed, a choice between two exceedingly under-dressed and over-bejewelled young women who were experts in the Art of Love.

He excused himself from this pleasure by saying how tired he was after his long journey.

It also meant that he left the Prince's Palace sooner than he had expected.

This was not before he had seen an amazing display of horsemanship.

Wild animals also were paraded in front of him, from what the Prince assured him was the most remarkable Zoo in Russia.

With some difficulty he managed to avoid accepting a variety of drugs which came from many different parts of the world, including China.

Using his perception, he knew when he left that he had exactly the answer the Prime Minister wanted.

From Yerevan he crossed the Russian border into Turkey.

He was now thinking of his own interests in wishing to see some rare Orchids which he was told grew on the Turkish mountains.

There was one in particular to be found on Mount Ararat.

The very day he arrived at Dogubavazit, Mount Ararat erupted.

It was not a very big eruption as eruptions go, but it caused a great commotion and frightened everyone in the nearby towns, including Dogubavazit.

The Duke was looked after with the greatest care by the Turks, who were proud that he should have visited their town.

Only a few of the inhabitants of the town were injured by falling rocks.

He was, however, interested to see how the Turks

coped with the eruptions which were known to occur frequently.

He went out while they were still collecting in the countryside at the foot of the mountain those who had been injured and taking them to hospital.

The dead were conveyed to a burial place.

The Duke, who could speak Turkish as well as many other languages, commiserated with those he met.

He understood how for many of them it meant not only the death of someone they loved, but also the ruination of the farm on which they depended for their livelihood.

But on the outskirts of the town a tragedy had occurred.

An Orphanage, set up originally by British Missionaries, had been almost completely demolished by a flow of lava.

Two children had been killed and three were injured.

The rest had managed to escape by taking refuge on a ridge of higher ground.

But now the woman in charge, who the Duke was to learn later had lost her husband, a Missionary, in a previous eruption, was in tears.

She was English and very relieved when the Duke spoke to her in her own language.

"What am I to do, Sir?" she asked. "What can I do? No-one in the town will want these children, and it took over three years to build the Mission."

Looking at it, the Duke saw there was little chance of saving anything.

It meant they would have to start again from scratch.

"Where did your children originally come from?" he asked.

"It was my husband's idea we should have the Mission here especially for children whose parents were killed by the eruptions which keep occurring."

She gave a little sob before she went on:

"No-one had ever thought of them before, and many just wandered about unattended in the Bazaar, begging for food from whoever was kind enough to take pity on them."

"And how many children have you got left?" the Duke asked.

Mrs. Winstead sighed.

"Twenty-four," she answered, "and where can I take them? Who will want twenty-four children?"

She suddenly thought he looked prosperous, and said quickly:

"Eleven of them are English. Their parents lost their lives climbing the mountain when they should have stayed at home. I can tell you, Sir, it is the children who suffer with no-one to love them and no-one to care."

It was then the Duke impulsively, because he was touched by Mrs. Winstead's misery, said:

"Take all the children to England and I will give you a house on my Estate. It will be better for them to be brought up there than struggling here to survive the eruptions which I understand continually take place."

He actually thought, although he did not say so, that it was rather foolish of them to build an Orphanage right below Mount Ararat.

At the same time, he felt strongly that something must be done about the orphans.

What he suggested seemed to be the only solution possible.

Mrs. Winstead could hardly believe her ears.

When she learned who he was, she was sure she must be dreaming.

The Duke took her and the children back to the town and found an Agent who would get them to a Black Sea port and from there arrange transport by sea to England.

"How can you be so kind?" Mrs. Winstead asked. "How can you have come at this moment when I was desperate, like an Arch-Angel from Heaven?"

"I am flattered you should think so," the Duke answered, "and I assure you they will be safer in England than they would be here."

Before he set off from home he made all the arrangements, and paid for the cost of the long voyage.

He knew that once he returned, it would be easy to tell his Manager at Stalbridge Hall to find a house for the orphans.

As it happened, he was to learn later that there was an empty house in the village.

It was big enough for the children and the elderly man who had lived there had just died.

He had been given the house, which was much too big for him, by the Duke's Father.

He had been the architect for the building of the new Stables of which the fourth Duke had been exceedingly proud.

The present Duke received regular reports about the orphans he had brought back to England from Turkey.

All of them were very satisfactory and he learnt they had settled in happily.

He had always meant to call on Mrs. Winstead.

But having been very pre-occupied in London, it always slipped his mind when he came to the Hall and he had never actually visited her.

He told himself now that perhaps this was the answer to his problem.

He only vaguely remembered the orphans, white-faced and frightened, when he had last seen them in Turkey.

Now he hoped there would be one amongst them who would be able to play the part he required.

'At least,' he thought bitterly, '*they* will be innocent and not perverted men like Prince Kaknovski.'

After what had occurred in his own house the previous night, the Duke knew that he would never trust anyone again.

He would certainly never believe that any woman, however young, was pure.

"This has made me decide once and for all that I will never get married," he told himself as he rode on. "If ever I do, it will not be until I am so old that if I am deceived again, it will not matter."

There was a bitterness and cynicism in his thoughts which had never been there before.

It made him feel as if he were waving a sabre at the ready to cut Lois and every woman like her into a thousand pieces.

He rode to the Orphanage which was at the far end of the village.

Outside it two boys were playing on the grass.

He asked them to look after his horse and see that it did not wander.

They were thrilled to do so.

The Duke then walked up to the front door and raised the knocker.

The rat-tat seemed to echo into what he thought must be quite a large Hall.

After some seconds the door was opened by Mrs. Winstead.

She looked at the Duke in surprise.

When he held out his hand, she realised who it was.

"Your Grace," she exclaimed, curtsying, "I had no idea it could be you."

"It may be rather early in the morning," the Duke replied, "but I particularly want to see you."

"Come in, please come in," Mrs. Winstead said in a flutter. "The children are just finishing their breakfast. I could not imagine who could be at the door."

She took the Duke into a comfortably furnished Sitting-Room on the other side of the Hall.

He thought at a quick glance that his Manager had furnished it well.

It was pleasant to look at, but at the same time appropriate for an Orphanage.

"I hope you are happy here, Mrs. Winstead," the Duke said.

"Ever so very happy, Your Grace, and everybody on your Estate has been kindness itself. In fact, I'm afraid sometimes they'll spoil the children."

"Let them be spoilt," the Duke said. "I am sure that is what they need, as they have no Father or Mother."

"They look very different now since you last saw them," Mrs. Winstead said. "But who could be anything but white with fright after what we had been through?"

"Who indeed?" the Duke agreed. "Now, Mrs. Winstead, I have come to see you to ask if you have an orphan in your charge who is seventeen or eighteen years of age."

Mrs. Winstead stared at him.

"Oh, no, Your Grace. The children I brought from Turkey were all very young. As you will remember, it was the younger parents who were climbing over the mountain and who got into trouble when it erupted, not the elderly."

The Duke had not thought of that.

"I had hoped," he said, "that you would have someone older amongst them."

Mrs. Winstead hesitated for a moment, and then she said:

"Well, there is one girl, Your Grace, about that age or maybe a little older."

"There is?" the Duke asked expectantly.

"Yes, it was after you left that they brought her down from the mountain, saying they had found her unconscious. She did not seem to be hurt, but she must have been concussed from a heavy fall."

The Duke was listening intently.

"What happened," he enquired.

"She had regained consciousness," Mrs. Winstead said, "but she had completely lost her memory."

"So she did not know who she was."

"No, Your Grace. She gave us no name, nor could she tell us anything about her family or why she was in Turkey."

"It seems strange," the Duke said. "Do you mean her memory has not yet come back to her?"

"No, Your Grace. It may seem that perhaps I was taking advantage of your kindness, but with twenty-four children to look after and some of them very young, I brought Zoe, as we call her, with us to England to help me."

"Zoe?" the Duke questioned.

"Well, it was a Greek man who found her and brought her down from the mountain," Mrs. Winstead explained, "and when he called the following day to see how she was, he asked her what her name was and what she had with her.

" 'I have nothing—nothing!' she replied, which was what she had said to me.

"The Greek man laughed and said: 'You have something, you are Zoe.' I am sure Your Grace knows that in Greek Zoe means Life."

The Duke was aware of this, and replied:

"It certainly seems an appropriate name, so Zoe is what she is called."

"She has not yet come up with a different name," Mrs. Winstead said. "Would Your Grace like to see her?"

"Yes, I would," the Duke answered.

Mrs. Winstead hurried from the room.

The Duke looked around, wondering what Zoe would be like.

It was too much to ask of his luck, or the Gods, that she should be suitable for him to present to his family.

If she was ugly, or in any way common-looking, then he would have to search elsewhere.

"Though God knows where," he murmured under his breath.

The door opened and Mrs. Winstead came back.

"Here is Zoe, Your Grace," she said.

Then, in what was meant to be a *sotto voce* tone but which was perfectly audible, she said:

"She's rather shy, not having met anyone like Your Grace before."

For a moment the Duke hardly dared to look at Zoe, feeling that so much rested on the appearance of this young woman.

Then, as she walked across the room behind Mrs. Winstead, he was aware that she was very slim.

She was walking with her head down, and over her hair she wore a piece of black cloth.

It was not unlike the veil of a Protestant Nun.

It struck him that perhaps that was what she was, though no-one might have thought of it.

Mrs. Winstead reached the Duke's side with Zoe just behind her.

Then from outside there was a sudden scream, as if a child had fallen down and hurt itself.

Zoe half-turned towards the door, but Mrs. Winstead said:

"I'll go, you stay here and talk to His Grace."

The scream came again as she hurried from the room.

The Duke looked at Zoe, whose head was still bent, and he said in a quiet voice:

"I expect Mrs. Winstead told you that I am the Duke of Stalbridge, and I am very interested to hear that you joined the party of orphans who came here from Dogubavazit."

There was silence, and then, as Zoe did not speak, the Duke went on:

"Would you oblige me by taking that black cloth off your head? I find it difficult to see you, and that is what I want to do."

For a moment Zoe did not move, and he thought she was going to refuse.

Then slowly she raised her arm and undid the cloth from the back of her head.

She pulled it off, and as she did so she looked at the Duke for the first time.

It was with the greatest difficulty that he did not give an audible gasp.

He was, in fact, speechless.

Facing him was a girl with a heart-shaped face

dominated by two dark eyes which seemed almost too large for it.

Her hair, which had been covered with the black cloth, was a gold he could never remember seeing before.

It was a deep shining gold which seemed to pick up the rays of the sunshine coming through the window.

There was just a touch of red in the curls which routed across her forehead.

He thought, in fact, he had never in the whole of his life seen anyone who looked so unusual.

Then, as he looked into her eyes, which were raised to his, he realised she was frightened.

With an effort, because he was surprised, he smiled at Zoe in a way that most women found irresistible and said:

"Now, that is better. It is easier to talk to you now I can see more than just the top of your head. Shall we sit down?"

He indicated the sofa that was in front of the fireplace.

As if he had given her an order, she sat on the edge of it, her hands in her lap.

The Duke sat in an armchair and said:

"I understand you have still not regained your memory."

"No, I remember ... nothing," Zoe said.

She spoke positively, but with just a tiny pause between the last two words, which made the Duke think she was perhaps not telling the truth.

"It must be very difficult for you," he said, "to have gone so long and still have no idea where you came from, who are your parents, or, for that matter, why you were on Mount Ararat."

Zoe made a graceful but helpless gesture with her hands.

"That is where they found me," she said.

"I am sure in most cases of concussion, if that is what you had," the Duke said, "the memory returns after days, weeks, or months. Surely sometimes you dream of different places from the one you are in now?"

"I remember . . . nothing," Zoe said again.

Now there was just a flicker in her dark eyes.

Using his perception, the Duke was quite certain she was lying.

He told himself, however, it did not matter whether she was telling the truth or not.

She was exactly what he wanted.

In fact, she exceeded his wildest expectations.

Settling himself a little more comfortably in the armchair, he said:

"Now, Zoe, I want your help."

"My help, Your Grace?"

She said the words quickly, as if she were frightened, and he answered:

"I came here thinking that one of the orphans might be old enough to do for me what I need, but Mrs. Winstead tells me they are all too young. So I am going to ask you to do something which will be of great help to me."

"I do not see how I can possibly help Your Grace," Zoe said.

"Wait until you have heard what I want," the Duke said.

He had not meant it to be a rebuke, but the colour came into her cheeks.

It made her look even lovelier than before.

How was it possible, he asked himself, that anything so beautiful could be hidden away in the Orphanage in his own village and no-one had told him about it.

Then he was sure that if ever she went out, she did not wish to be noticed.

Zoe, therefore, wore the dark veil over her hair which made her look like a Protestant Nun.

The question was, why did she not wish to be noticed?

The Duke was intrigued, but at the same time he told himself first things first, and he must solve his own problem.

"Now, what I want you to do, Zoe," he said, "is to come to my house, which, of course, you know, to-morrow night and have Dinner with me."

Zoe's eyes opened so wide in surprise that they were even larger than they had been before.

"Have Dinner with Your Grace?" she repeated. "But I could . . . not do . . . that!"

"Why not?" the Duke asked.

She hesitated before she said:

"I have . . . nothing to . . . wear."

The Duke smiled.

"That will be attended to. You will be given a gown to wear. All you have to do is to sit at the table, eat your Dinner, and talk to those on either side of you."

"Why do I have to do this?" Zoe asked.

"Because it will help me," the Duke said.

There was silence while he fought for words, and then he said:

"I have been put in a very ignominious position. In fact, I have been caught in a trap which will make me very unhappy if I cannot escape from it."

Zoe was listening, and now with a look of interest in her eyes she asked:

"What sort of trap?"

"There is someone whom I asked to marry me, but I have just discovered that she accepted me, not because she loves me," the Duke answered, "but because I am a Duke and a rich man."

To his surprise, he saw a faint smile on Zoe's lips.

As if he could read her thoughts, he knew she was thinking that was an inevitable situation where a man like himself was concerned.

Yet how could she know that, and how indeed could she think it? he asked himself.

"I suppose I should tell you," he went on, "that my family are all coming to stay with me, and they believe that I will tell them at Dinner tomorrow what they have wanted to hear for a long time, that I am to marry so that I can have an heir. But, as I have just told you, it is now impossible for me to marry the girl whom I had intended to marry."

He realised that Zoe was puzzling a little over this.

However, she did not ask any questions, and he continued:

"What I want therefore is to produce you, who are unknown and who no-one realises even exists, and tell them that you are my choice. There will then be no question of my marrying this other girl."

"And what . . . will happen . . . then?" Zoe asked nervously.

"When they have all left my house, you can return to the Orphanage and forget what has happened," the Duke said. "I shall be very grateful to you, and there will be no need for me to bother you again."

"And you do not . . . intend ever to be . . . married?" Zoe said.

She obviously found it hard to understand exactly what he envisaged happening.

"I will not marry anyone for at least the next twenty years," the Duke said, and now his voice was firm. "I hope that what you will do for me will ensure that I am left alone in the future and not pushed and badgered by people who will not mind their own business."

He could not help his anger swelling up.

To Zoe his voice seemed to vibrate round the room.

"And that is . . . all I . . . have to . . . do?" she asked.

"It is no more than acting a charade," the Duke said.

Then he wondered if in her circumstances Zoe had ever taken part in a charade, or even had any idea what it was.

Because she was looking worried, he said:

"I promise it will be very easy for you. I shall be standing beside you all the time and, after I have introduced you, we will leave the Dining-Room and go to the Ball-Room. You can have just one dance with me and then go straight to bed."

He saw that Zoe was twisting her fingers together as if she were worried.

"What is frightening you?" he asked gently. "I saw you were frightened when you came in, and I thought it strange that anyone should be afraid of me."

"I am not . . . frightened of you," Zoe said.

"Then why are you frightened?"

He knew before she spoke that she was not going to tell him.

"I do not know," she said. "Perhaps it is because I cannot remember. But of course it is very stupid of me and I am quite safe in England."

The Duke was suddenly alert.

Safe from what?

It was quite out of context in this particular conversation, and he was certain it meant something very special to Zoe.

He was, however, far too experienced to let her know he had noticed that she might have made a slip.

Instead, he said:

"Just trust me and leave everything to me. I will tell you what I want now, and then you need not even think about it again until I send a carriage for you at seven o'clock tomorrow evening."

"What shall I . . . wear?" Zoe asked.

"That is a very feminine question," the Duke said as he smiled, "which I was just going to answer. I want you to give me a dress which fits you so that the dress in which you perform, and do not forget you are acting a part, will fit you and look exactly how I want you to look."

"Shall I go and get it now?" Zoe enquired.

"Yes, do that, and our conversation, Zoe, is entirely private. I will tell Mrs. Winstead I am sending for you tomorrow night, but there is no reason for her to know why, or for you to tell her anything that I have told you about my situation. That is private."

"Of course," Zoe said, "I understand that."

She stood up, and then she said:

"I will try not to fail Your Grace. I do not want to do this but, if I can help you after you have helped me by bringing me here to England, then of course I must do what you want."

"I want it very much, Zoe," the Duke said, "and I know you will look the part. When they see you, no-one will be the least surprised at what I announce."

"At the same time, I am very frightened," Zoe said. "So please, if I make a mistake, you must not be very angry."

"You will not make a mistake, and I will not be

angry," the Duke promised. "Just trust me, and I feel that fate, or perhaps the Gods themselves, has brought you to me when I need you so desperately."

"I hope that is true," Zoe said, "and it is what I felt when I stepped off the ship that had brought me to England."

There was a little note which again sounded like fear in her voice which the Duke did not miss.

There was something about Zoe which told him that her case was not as plain sailing as Mrs. Winstead believed.

There was something behind all this, something very strange which the Duke was determined to unravel.

"She needs help," he told himself.

At the same time, it seemed incredible that looking as she did and being obviously well-bred, he should have found her when he most needed her.

"Go and get the dress I want," he said gently. "If you pack it in a parcel, there will be no reason for Mrs. Winstead to know what it contains."

"I am afraid it is only a dress I made myself," Zoe explained. "You see, I had nothing . . . when I was . . . picked up on the . . . mountainside."

"Nothing except Zoe," the Duke said with a smile.

She smiled back at him.

He thought it made her even more fantastically beautiful than when she looked serious.

Then, with her golden hair glittering, she ran from the room to do what he had told her.

chapter three

WHEN the Duke got back to the Hall, he sent for his Housekeeper.

Mrs. Partridge had been there ever since he had been a small boy, and she came hurrying to find out what he required.

"I need your help, Mrs. Partridge," the Duke said. "Have we still got a seamstress?"

"Of course, Your Grace," Mrs. Partridge replied almost reproachfully. "Miss Lawson has been with us for over twenty years."

"Then please fetch her," the Duke said, "because I need you both for something very urgent."

Mrs. Partridge hurried away, and after a short time came back with Miss Lawson.

She was a rather withered-looking little woman.

But the Duke remembered his Mother had always said what a good seamstress she was, and how it would be impossible to run the house without her.

The Duke shook her hand and said how nice it was to see her again.

Miss Lawson, bobbing him a curtsy, was delighted.

"Now I want you both to listen to what I require," he said. "I have coming here for Dinner tomorrow evening a young lady who is doing me a great favour. So I want everything you do for her to be perfect."

He knew both the elderly women were looking at him attentively, and he went on:

"Miss Zoe, for that is her name, is very young and very beautiful, and I want her to appear at my party tomorrow night looking if possible more like a Greek goddess than a young girl."

Both Mrs. Partridge and Miss Lawson gave little gasps, but they did not interrupt.

"I have here," the Duke said, bringing forward the parcel Zoe had given him, "one of the dresses she made herself which therefore fits her exactly. What I require by tomorrow evening is a gown of dazzling white resembling those worn by the Goddesses whose statues are in the alcoves in the Hall, or I can easily find you an illustration of one in the Library."

Mrs. Partridge looked anxiously at Miss Lawson.

"Do we have any such white material, Miss Lawson?" she asked.

Miss Lawson was thinking.

"I'm sure we have," she said, "in the attic where we put away Her Grace's materials which had never been used."

The Duke gave a sigh of relief.

"Then that is settled," he said, "but I think Miss Zoe will also require something to wear on Sunday."

He was thinking as he spoke.

It was obvious that the Minfordburys would leave

very early on Sunday without, he hoped, speaking to him.

But the rest of the Party would doubtless linger on, some at least expecting to have Luncheon before they left for their own homes.

With his usual eye for detail he was aware that Zoe would have nothing to wear on Sunday except, as she had said, clothes she had made herself.

They would probably seem rather surprising if they followed the gown that he had ordered for her to wear on Saturday.

"I would not, Your Grace, be able to make two gowns by tomorrow evening," Miss Lawson said apologetically.

"I can understand that," the Duke said, "but perhaps we have something in the house."

He looked at Mrs. Partridge as he spoke.

"There are, of course, Her Grace's gowns," she replied, "which His Grace, your Father, told us to put away in wardrobes that were not being used, and they've been there ever since."

"I am sure you can find something suitable for Miss Zoe," the Duke suggested.

He thought as he spoke that his Mother would have been only too willing to help him escape from a marriage which for him would be nothing but a farce.

Even to think of Lois and her behaviour brought his anger back, and it obviously showed on his face.

Mrs. Partridge said quickly:

"I'm sure, Your Grace, that Miss Lawson and I will not fail you. While she's making the white gown, I'll find something suitable for this young lady to wear at Luncheon on Sunday. And of course she may need a hat."

"I will leave you to think of everything," the Duke

said in a lofty manner. "But I assure you it is most important that she should look exactly right, first for the Dinner-Party tomorrow night and secondly for Luncheon on Sunday."

He left the room and the two women looked at each other in consternation.

"It's going to be a difficult job to get everything done so quickly," Miss Lawson said apprehensively.

"I'll give you Mabel to help you," Mrs. Partridge replied. "She's an intelligent girl, and I think you'll find you can trust her to do exactly what you tell her."

Miss Lawson picked up the package which contained Zoe's gown.

"It seems to me," she said as she did so, "somewhat strange that His Grace has another young lady coming to Dinner. I hears, although I understands it's a secret, that he's going to announce his engagement to Lady Lois."

"I hope he's going to do nothing of the sort," Mrs. Partridge said tartly. "She may be pretty, but beauty that's only skin deep is not good enough for Stalbridge Hall."

She spoke in a manner which told Miss Lawson there was something she knew which other people did not.

As they walked down the corridor together, Miss Lawson was asking questions to which she hoped Mrs. Partridge would give her an answer.

The Duke had gone to his Study feeling that he was more fortunate than he had dared to anticipate.

He could still hardly believe that Zoe was as overwhelmingly beautiful as she revealed after removing the veil she had worn on her head.

Thinking it over, the Duke knew he had never seen a more beautiful woman.

But she was not in the least like any other Beauty he had known.

There was something very different about her, something that told him that she was not entirely English.

She certainly spoke English perfectly and was well educated.

There was no doubt that her hair and her white skin could be attributed to traditional English Beauty.

But her eyes did not fit into the picture.

They were also extremely sensitive, so he could almost read her thoughts by watching one look following another.

He knew, looking back over the many women he had known, that he had never seen such strange eyes on an English woman.

At the same time, he could not put a name to a foreign country from which they might have come.

"She is a mystery," he told himself, and knew he was intensely curious about her.

He was also exceedingly grateful that she should have appeared just when he needed her so desperately.

She was exactly what he required to surprise his family and to perplex and infuriate Lois.

Once again he was feeling enraged that she had managed so deftly to deceive him.

He knew it was something he would never be able to forget or to forgive.

The Duke had been up so early that he had nearly finished his Breakfast before Charles and the Marquess appeared.

It was understood at Stalbridge Hall that the Ladies should Breakfast in their bedrooms or in Boudoirs which were attached to most of the more important rooms.

Charles and the Marquess came in together.

The Duke hastily finished his cup of coffee and rose to his feet.

"I hope you will forgive me if I hurry away," he said, "but I still have a great deal to arrange about the Point-to-Point, and about the hedges which have to be erected later in the afternoon."

"Do you want me to come and help you?" Charles asked.

By this time the Duke had reached the door.

"I am not quite certain where I shall be," he replied.

Charles looked after him questioningly.

Knowing the Duke so well, he was aware as soon as he came into the Breakfast-Room that something was wrong.

He supposed it was just some order which had not been carried out.

Perhaps one of the horses in which he was particularly interested had sprained a fetlock.

At the same time, it was unlike the Duke not to tell him what had upset him.

He wanted to hurry after him, but there was really no point in doing so until he had eaten his breakfast.

While doing so he had to listen to the Marquess droning on about the difficulties of rising expenses, especially when it concerned horses.

Charles was not particularly sympathetic.

The Marquess was looking forward to the future, when he could be sure of help and support from his son-in-law in all his difficulties.

When a little later in the morning Charles went to look for the Duke, he could not find him.

Because the Duke did not wish to talk to Charles,

he had mounted another horse and set off to ride on a part of his Estate that he had not visited for some time.

When he was coming back, it was getting on for Luncheon time.

It was then that he told himself he would like to have another talk with Zoe.

He was wondering if he had made a mistake and she was not really as beautiful as she had seemed to him early that morning.

'Perhaps I was blinded by the shock of what happened last night,' he thought, 'or just grasping at any straw to save me from drowning!'

Then he tried to laugh at himself for making a mountain out of a molehill.

But he knew it was all too true that where he was concerned, it was very much a mountain.

Thinking of mountains, he wondered how it was possible for Zoe to have been so heavily concussed that her memory had still not come back.

Could she really have forgotten the years in which she had grown up from a child to a young woman?

Was there some reason for her to say continually that she could not remember.

He had ridden quite a way from the house.

By the time he returned he realised he no longer felt embarrassed at meeting Charles or Minfordbury.

He had only to see the carriages that were following one after another up the long drive to know that many of his relatives were already arriving.

He had left it more or less up to them whether they arrived on Friday or Saturday.

He had forgotten that to be invited to Stalbridge Hall was for them always an excitement.

Those who received an invitation were determined

to make the very most of it.

When he dismounted outside the front door, it was to find half-a-dozen of his relations in the hall.

They had just arrived and the Drawing-Room seemed almost over-crowded with others.

They were all talking at once, asking him questions and enquiring specially why the Party was being held.

Everyone told the Duke over and over again how delighted they were to be with him.

It was fortunate there were enough footmen to carry the luggage upstairs.

Even more fortunately there were enough rooms to accommodate them all in the greatest comfort.

The Duke had a superlative memory, which enabled him to say:

"I have given you your favourite room, Aunt Patricia, and I know, Cousin Cecilia, you always like the room which overlooks the rose-garden."

They were all touched and delighted that he had remembered them.

What they did not know was that his Mother had kept a record of the likes and dislikes of the family who continually visited them.

In fact, the Duke had often laughed at it with Charles and enjoyed such entries as:

'Cousin Matilda wants three blankets and a hot drink of honey with just a touch of rum in it last thing at night.'

There was, the Duke thought, an even funnier one recording that Uncle Harold wished his shaving-water to be nearly boiling and four pillows besides the bolster on his bed.

"Does he sit up all night?" Charles had asked when he read it.

"No, he lies on them," the Duke explained. "He

says no mattress is as comfortable as a pillow, and therefore he insists that he is provided with pillows on which he can really sleep in comfort."

There were all sorts of amusing notes in the book.

It made it easy for the Duke to seem to be taking particular care with each one of his relatives.

He also noticed that when Lois appeared she was making herself very pleasant to the new arrivals.

His Uncles particularly were delighted with her.

His young Cousins made a bee-line for her as soon as they came into the room.

The Duke could not help thinking cynically that if he married her, he would always be wondering with which man she was "having an affair" as soon as he was out of the house.

At least a dozen times during the day, when he watched Lois looking so young and innocent moving about among the older generation, he told himself he would never marry.

'All women are untrustworthy,' he thought, 'and I have no intention of being cuckolded by any man, whether friend or foe.'

He knew also that if he were married, he would never allow himself to be made to look a fool.

Inevitably, sooner or later he would have to fight a duel with some man who he believed had insulted him.

He had fought one duel in his life.

He had won, and the man who had challenged him went about with his arm in a sling for two months.

The Duke had felt it was unfair.

He knew he was in the wrong and he should have suffered.

He was, however, too good a shot to lose a duel no matter how expert his opponent might be.

All the afternoon people kept arriving, which made it impossible to do anything but greet them.

There was for the Duke still quite a lot to arrange for the Point-to-Point.

The men who were mapping out the route kept consulting him.

A swollen stream had made one place impassable which had been used the previous year.

In another part of the course the fields had been newly sown with corn.

The riders had therefore to be redirected.

Finally all the flags were in place.

The winning-post was set up with plenty of seating erected alongside.

The ladies not taking part would be able to watch the triumphant finish of the victor.

The Duke never rode in his own Point-to-Point.

He helped the Stewards by keeping watch to see that no-one cheated, and of course presented the prizes as soon as the race was over.

He had intended, when he originally organised the party, that on Friday night he would make an opportunity to talk quietly and intimately with Lois.

He wanted to take her into the Garden and show her his Orchids.

Now he knew he had to provide some sort of entertainment both for the Party and to keep himself busily occupied.

As the majority of his Guests were middle-aged or elderly, he told the Servants to put up the card-tables.

There was also a roulette-wheel which he had brought back from Monte Carlo.

He had thought it might be amusing sometimes to gamble at home when he had a male Party.

He was, however, not surprised when the ladies

and even his Grandmother, said they would like to have a flutter.

He had wisely brought the whole equipment including a lot of pretence money which they preferred to the usual chips.

After what was an excellent Dinner they all crowded into the Music-Room.

From the laughter that Charles caused when he declared he had broken the bank, the Duke knew that the evening was a success.

He was aware that Lois was looking at him from time to time.

He guessed she was surprised he was not at her side or making suggestions to take her where they could be alone.

The Duke, however, had had a great deal of experience in avoiding women who were chasing him.

He therefore managed that it should appear quite natural that he had other duties to attend to.

When it was time to go to bed, he realised he had not spoken one single word to her since early in the afternoon.

He thought bitterly that it would not perturb her very much, as it would give her another chance of being with Charles.

It was what he had heard her beg for last night.

It was only Charles who realised he was not his usual self.

As they had a nightcap before they went upstairs, he said:

"Are you all right, old boy?"

"What do you mean by that?" the Duke enquired.

"I just had the idea you were not quite up to scratch, but I hope I am mistaken."

"I have had quite a lot to worry me today," the Duke said enigmatically.

He did not wait for Charles to reply and walked away.

He had no idea his friend was staring after him with a puzzled expression in his eyes.

When Charles realised there was nothing he could do about it, he shrugged his shoulders and went upstairs.

The Duke was in no hurry to try to go to sleep.

He was still suffering in the same way he had suffered the night before, knowing he had been betrayed, deceived, and humiliated.

He decided that as soon as the Season was over he would go abroad.

When travelling, at least he would not be bothered by people trying to force him into marriage.

There were amusements and delights in all the Capital cities in Europe which were not obtainable in England.

Yet what he really enjoyed was being alone on long treks which took him to the top of some obscure mountain or towards the horizon of a waterless desert.

"I will travel," the Duke declared, "and the Social world can do without me as I can do without it."

He spoke almost savagely.

He was aware, although the knowledge annoyed him, that he was still hurt because his dreams had failed him and he no longer believed in love.

"There is no such thing," he told himself. "It is all an illusion thought up by foolish women and beardless boys."

It was far better to believe in Prince Kaknovski and

his perversions which were more true to human nature.

Because he was hating the whole world, he had a strong drink before he went to bed, which was something he seldom did.

The next day was hustle and bustle from the moment the Duke woke.

When he was called he was informed that one of the grooms in charge of the horses had been taken ill during the night.

A horse belonging to a Guest had run wild and knocked down some of the fencing.

One of his neighbours who always acted as a judge at this particular Point-to-Point had sent a message to say he had a high temperature and was unable to come.

The Duke was expected to put everything to rights from the moment he came downstairs to Breakfast.

He did his best.

That the Point-to-Point started only ten minutes late, with the full number of runners that they had expected, was due entirely to his genius for organisation.

Charles, who was riding one of his best horses, said to the Duke:

"I hope you are backing me, Ivor. I was, although you may not have noticed it, extremely abstemious last night."

"Then you certainly ought to come in first on this animal," the Duke said.

He patted the horse which he had bought at Tattersall's a year ago at an extremely high price.

He did not meet his friend's eyes.

As Charles rode off to the starting-point, he wondered once again what had upset him.

It never occurred to him that the Duke might have discovered his liaison with Lois.

It had in fact already existed for some months before the Duke met her, and Charles was not her first lover.

The Duke had been so difficult about marriage and had never been interested in any young girls.

But when Charles saw that the Duke was attracted to Lois, he had thought she would in fact make him a very good wife.

She was beautiful, there was no doubt about that.

She came from an excellent family, which should please the Duke's relations.

She was intelligent enough to play any particular part that was expected of her.

She had very cleverly presented herself as a young and innocent girl, which Charles knew the Duke would find unusual and intriguing.

She was at the same time quite capable of being a good hostess as the Duchess of Stalbridge both in London and the country.

She had been well brought up.

She knew that she must call on the farmers and on the pensioners in the almshouses, open the Flower Show, and give away the prizes at the local School.

In fact, Charles had calculated it would be difficult for the Duke, however fastidious he might be, to find fault with her as his wife.

Yet as he waited for the signal for the race to start, Charles was worried.

The Duke did not seem like himself, and he could not imagine what could be upsetting him.

The race started and Charles was aware from the moment it did so that he was riding the best horse of the twenty-eight entries.

He also knew the course because he had ridden on it before.

Holding back his horse, he settled down to make sure this time he won the race.

The Exhibition of jumping in the afternoon was something the Duke inaugurated some years ago.

It was a most popular entertainment for the villagers to watch and for those who had a decent horse with which to compete.

While they were having Luncheon, the fences were arranged near the winning-post of the Point-to-Point.

It was in itself a small race-course.

Because he enjoyed jumping, the Duke took part in this.

He could easily have been the winner but avoided that by not taking the last jump the third time the riders went round the course.

There were three falls, but no-one was hurt.

A horse got stuck in the middle of a fence which caused a great deal of amusement.

When the afternoon ended, everyone said they had never enjoyed themselves so much.

They all went up to shake the Duke by the hand before they left.

When he finally could go back to the Hall, it was time to have his bath before Dinner.

He had, however, as he was well aware, something important to do first.

He had given his Coachman explicit orders as to the time at which he should collect Zoe, and to which door he should take her.

The side-door was seldom used.

When the carriage drew up outside it, the Duke himself opened the door.

As Zoe stepped out, for a moment he wondered if

he had made a terrible mistake.

She was wearing the same plain cotton dress she had been wearing yesterday.

Her hair was covered with the black veil in which he had first seen her.

Then, as she looked up at him, he saw her eyes.

Whatever she was wearing, he knew she was the most beautiful woman he had ever seen and quite the most unusual.

"You have come," he said. "I was half afraid you would run away at the last moment."

Zoe smiled.

"I must confess I thought of ... doing so ... because I ... am so ... frightened."

"You are not to be frightened," the Duke said. "Everything is planned and I shall be angry not with you, but only with myself, if anything goes wrong."

"Now you have ... definitely made me more ... frightened than I was ... before," Zoe said.

There was just a little touch of humour in her voice, which amused the Duke.

He took her up the side staircase which led to the first landing.

At the end of it there was the Master Suite.

He had deliberately put Zoe in one of the State Rooms which was not being used.

It was unlikely that any of his other Guests would see her in this part of the house.

There was only his Grandmother, his Aunt Margaret, and another Uncle and Aunt in the State Rooms.

They were all too old, the Duke thought, with the exception of his Grandmother, to be particularly curious about other people.

Nor were they interested in matters which did not concern themselves.

In the State Room to which he took Zoe, Mrs. Partridge and Miss Lawson were waiting.

The Duke could not help noticing the consternation in Mrs. Partridge's face when she first saw Zoe, then the astonishment in her eyes when Zoe removed her black veil and revealed her extraordinary gold hair.

The Duke introduced Mrs. Partridge and Miss Lawson to her, and then he said:

"My Housekeeper and my seamstress have been working very hard to have a gown ready for you, and if you will let me know when you have changed, I want to bring you something to wear round your neck."

"I do not . . . expect I will . . . take very . . . long," Zoe replied.

The Duke left then and went to his own room.

His bath was ready and his Valet was waiting to help him into his evening-clothes.

Hubert had been with the Duke in India as his batman and had travelled with him ever since.

Sometimes, when the Duke was on some particular mission, Hubert had been left with the luggage to wait for his Master's return.

Although the Duke had not been aware of it, Hubert worried over him.

He was terrified that without him the Duke might have an accident or, what was more likely, be injured or killed by an enemy.

As he dressed, the Duke said:

"What I want you to do, Hubert, is to bring Miss Zoe downstairs into the Drawing-Room exactly one minute before Dawson announces that Dinner is ready."

"I understands, Your Grace," Hubert replied. "You can trust me to get her there promptly."

"I know that," the Duke said. "As you and I have often said before, it is just a matter of timing."

They laughed.

They both remembered occasions when the right timing had been a matter of life or death.

When the Duke was ready, he collected something from his wash-stand which had been lying in the basin which was filled with ice.

He attached it to a collet of small diamonds and walked to the room next door.

He knocked and Mrs. Partridge called: "Come in, Your Grace."

Zoe was standing by the Dressing-Table.

When he looked at her he knew she far exceeded his expectation and was more effective than he had dared to hope.

The gown Miss Lawson had made for her was of a soft material, and was so extremely white it might have been a sheath of newly fallen snow.

Just as the Duke had asked, it was designed in the classic style portrayed in so many Greek statues.

It showed off Zoe's long neck.

Her arms were bare and the bodice fitted tightly.

The skirt seemed to fall almost as if by a master hand, softly in front and reaching the floor at the back.

It was the sort of dress that might have been worn by Aphrodite or Diana of the Chase.

The only touch of colour was Zoe's extraordinary golden hair which framed her heart-shaped face.

It seemed as if it shimmered and glittered in the light from the candles to accentuate the darkness of her huge eyes.

For a moment the Duke could only stare at her without moving.

Then, as he went forward, he said:

"I congratulate you, Miss Lawson. In France they would hail you as a genius!"

"I'm glad Your Grace is pleased," Miss Lawson said as she smiled.

The Duke turned to Zoe.

"I have here," he said, "something I want you to wear round your neck."

Zoe looked at it and gave a little cry.

"Oh, it is an Orchid!"

"It is the *Chusua Donii*," the Duke said, "which comes from Tibet, and it is the first time this Orchid has ever blossomed outside its own country."

Zoe looked again and realised it was attached to a chain of diamonds.

"Suppose I damage it?" she asked.

"I feel sure you will not do that," the Duke answered, "and it is only right you should wear it."

Very gently he fastened the diamond collet at the back of her neck.

He knew that if Miss Lawson had been a genius in carrying out his order, he himself had been a genius in giving the flower.

"I am now going downstairs," he said. "Soon my Valet will collect you and bring you to where I will be waiting. Just come straight to me and I will take you into Dinner."

He saw that Zoe was following everything he said and was making a mental note of it.

Then, as he looked at her again, he found it hard to believe that she was real.

He went from the room without saying another word.

Downstairs the Drawing-Room was filled with the relations who were staying with him and those from neighbouring houses.

The Duke greeted the new-comers.

They told him how exciting it was to be at Stal-bridge Hall.

"It is just like the old days," more than one of them said, "when your Mother used to arrange such beautiful Parties for us."

"And that is what I must try to do in the future," the Duke said.

He realised that although he spoke for himself, there was a knowing look in some of his relations' eyes.

They thought it would be his wife who would be doing that in the future.

The Duke had spent some time in re-arranging the seating at table exactly as he now wanted it.

He thought as he looked round the Drawing-Room that it would be almost impossible to seat one more guest in the Dining-Room, large though it was.

"They are all here," he told himself, "and now let battle commence."

He moved towards the door.

He had not reached it when Zoe came in.

Only those who were nearest the Duke saw her, and they were suddenly silent.

It was as if they found it hard to believe what they were seeing.

Walking with a grace the Duke had not expected, she moved towards him almost as if her small feet did not touch the floor.

He took her outstretched hand and raised it in the French fashion to his lips.

As he did so, Dawson announced with a stentorian voice:

"Dinner is served, Your Grace."

The Duke offered Zoe his right arm.

She put her fingers just inside it.

He was surprised that she knew the right way to do so, as he realised it was something he had forgotten to tell her.

Without looking back, they moved slowly down the corridor which led to the Dining-Room.

The Duke was aware that his relatives were following them, but not very quickly, as some of the older women had to be helped to their feet and this delayed the procession a little.

In the Dining-Room the table was glittering with gold candelabra and goblets which had been fashioned by famous goldsmiths down the centuries.

The only thing missing was flowers.

The Duke's Mother had always insisted these were arranged round the base of the candelabra and the Sèvres dishes which contained fruit.

Tonight the Duke was determined they should concentrate on one flower and one flower only.

He took Zoe to her place which was on the left of the high chair on which he himself sat at the top of the table.

His Grandmother, the Dowager Duchess, was on his right hand.

He was aware as he sat down that Lois was staring in bewilderment at the seating-plan.

It was on a small table just inside the door.

She had, of course, expected to be sitting beside him.

Instead, he had put her at the far end of the table, which was actually a place of honour.

It was where at Dinner-Parties his Mother had always sat.

He had thought this out rather cruelly.

Lois, though surprised, would think in finding herself in such an important position, that it was a privilege.

She was therefore smiling as she seated herself with an Earl on one side of her and Charles on the other.

It was Charles who was looking perplexed.

He had gone over the seating-plan with the Duke before they left London.

There had been no word then of an extra Guest who was not, as far as he knew, one of the Stalbridge family.

"Who is she?" he asked himself.

He knew the same question was being whispered amongst the other Guests at the table.

All of them seemed compelled to look to where a golden head was glinting against the dark panelling behind it.

Dinner started and the Chefs had really excelled themselves.

Even the Duke had to admit he had seldom tasted better food or more unusual dishes.

There was Champagne to drink and then a very unusual and excellent white wine.

Finally after the dessert, Champagne glasses were once again put on the table.

Everyone was sure they were now about to drink the health of their Host and future wife.

The Duke did not rise until the Servants had left the room.

Then, getting to his feet, he said:

"This is a very exciting and unusual occasion, first because I want to welcome you all here tonight and to tell you how delightful it is for me to entertain you in my own house.''

There were murmurs of applause at this, and the Duke went on:

''But there is another reason why this is a very special occasion. It is because I have with me someone you have not yet met, but who in my opinion is one of the most interesting, unusual, and original young women I have ever known, beside being much the most beautiful.''

He looked down for a moment at Zoe as he spoke.

After a surprised silence, one or two of the men murmured, ''Hear, hear.''

''The lady I am talking about,'' the Duke went on, ''has only one name. It is Zoe. Those of you who learnt any Greek at School or University will remember that Zoe is the Greek for 'Life.' It is the only name she has.''

He looked down at her and smiled, then continued:

''She was found, heavily concussed, lying on the mountain-side after an eruption of Mount Ararat in Turkey, and she has not yet regained her memory. A Greek man who discovered her asked who she was and where she came from, and when she told him she did not know, she added: 'I have nothing ... nothing.' ''

'' 'You have life,' he said, and he used the Greek word 'Zoe.' Zoe therefore is her name, and I think she must be unique in that she has started a new life without any regrets, or any worries or memories of the past.''

He paused and then continued:

''Life to her is new and exciting, and the years she has lived before do not exist. That in itself is amazing. Tonight, when I asked Zoe to come here, I gave her to wear something as unique as herself. It is the Orchid *Chusua Donii*, which for the first time ever has blossomed outside its own country, which is Tibet, and has managed to survive in a world that is not many thousands of feet high. So, Ladies and Gentlemen, I bring to your notice a living woman and a living plant, each of them unique and exceptionally beautiful. And I ask you to drink a toast to Zoe and to me that we may find happiness together."

As he finished speaking, the Duke put down his hand and drew Zoe up beside him.

For a moment they just stood there.

They knew the silence was because the Duke had astonished and stunned his audience into what was almost immobility.

Then several of the men recovered, and rising to their feet they lifted their glasses; slowly the women joined them.

"Good health! Good luck!" The words were repeated over and over again.

Then the Duke, giving his arm to Zoe, walked slowly from the Dining-Room.

Only as they passed through the door to find Dawson waiting on the other side of it did he say:

"Announce that there is dancing in the Ball-Room."

"Very good, Your Grace," Dawson replied.

The Duke and Zoe walked down the corridor aware that no-one yet was following them.

When they reached the hall, Zoe said in a small voice:

"That was a very . . . clever . . . speech."

"I hoped you would think so," the Duke answered.

They walked on a little further, and she looked at the staircase and said:

"Do you . . . want me to . . . go now?"

"No, of course not," the Duke answered. "I explained to you before that you must not only stay the night but remain here until all my Guests have left."

"But how can I do . . . that when I have . . . nothing to . . . wear?"

"I have arranged for that," the Duke answered. "Miss Lawson, who made this dress for you, will have another ready tomorrow morning."

To his surprise, she laughed.

It was a very pretty laugh, something he had not heard before.

"I thought I was dreaming," she said, "but now I know you are a Magician and where you are concerned anything is possible!"

chapter four

As they entered the Ball-Room the band was playing a dreamy Waltz.

The Duke put his arm around Zoe and started to move slowly round the polished floor.

The Ball-Room was decorated with white pillars picked out in gold and had a large mural of Venice at one end of the room.

There were three French windows opening out into the Garden.

A mass of plants and flowers decorated the stage on which the band was playing.

The Duke had wondered if Zoe could dance, having no idea what sort of family or country she came from.

But as soon as they had taken a few steps, he realised she was as light as thistledown.

She moved rhythmically with him almost as if they were one person dancing rather than two.

It was not long before the younger members of the

Duke's family came into the Ball-Room and joined them on the floor.

They were giggling and exchanging glances with each other, and the Duke wondered if it was at his expense.

He and Zoe danced without speaking until, when he thought the Waltz was coming to an end, he stopped.

He said as he did so:

"Would you like to go into the Garden?"

He wanted to avoid the questions he was quite certain every one of his family would want to ask him.

Zoe, without replying, walked towards one of the open windows and stepped out into the starlight.

When the Duke joined her, she said:

"I think what we really ought to do is to put your beautiful Orchid, which you attached to my necklace, back in the greenhouse. I do not want it to die."

The Duke thought this was a good idea, and they walked across the lawn towards the shrubbery.

He was aware as he did so that Zoe was looking up at the stars.

Then she seemed fascinated by the moonlight shining on the lake and on the small cascade on the other side of the lawn.

When they reached the greenhouse, the Duke opened the door and lighted a lantern.

As usual, he felt a little thrill at seeing the colours of the Orchids that were in flower, and thinking how beautifully they blended in with each other.

To his surprise, Zoe was silent.

Everyone he took to see his Orchids began to gush almost before they went through the door.

"How pretty! How beautiful! How clever of you!

They are charming! What a pity they have so little scent."

The Duke thought he had heard the words repeated and repeated until they almost haunted him because they were inevitably the same.

Zoe, however, said nothing.

She merely stood, looking round her almost if she were spellbound.

Then he was aware she was concentrating on each Orchid separately.

She spent a long time look at the *Laeliocattleya*, whose purple flowers were in full bloom.

The Duke thought they looked magnificent, as if they deliberately lorded it over their less spectacular neighbours.

Then Zoe turned to each of the other plants.

The Duke thought that the yellow of the *Cymbidium* was not as golden as her hair.

She still did not say anything.

Only after she appeared to have finished did he opened the door into the next greenhouse.

None of these Orchids were in bloom, and Zoe did not hesitate.

She moved to the far end of the greenhouse as if she were drawn to what was waiting there.

Two more *Chusua Donii* plants were in bud and matching the snowy white of the dress that she wore.

She looked at them wide-eyed.

The Duke felt as if he heard her say a thousand words of appreciation without a sound passing her lips.

Then she looked up at him.

He knew she was waiting for him to take the Orchid she wore from around her neck.

She bent her head.

Very gently he undid the diamond collet and she held it in both her hands.

The Duke was aware that even though the Orchid had been away from the ice, and in the warmth of the Dining-Room and the Ball-Room, it did not seem to have damaged the flower.

Carefully he removed it from where he had fastened it to the necklace.

He put it between two of the blocks of ice.

It was then Zoe spoke for the first time.

"I think it knows," she said softly, "how important it has been tonight and how everyone is terribly impressed that . . . you have . . . grown it in . . . this climate."

"I have done my best," the Duke said, "to make the *Chusua Donii* feel at home."

As he spoke, from beside the large bowl which held the Orchid and the ice he picked up a fan.

It was one he had bought in Japan.

Of very thin delicately made paper, it created a draught that was stronger than anything that could be produced by satin or lace.

"The Garden boys," he explained, "on my instructions, fan the plant every morning and evening so that my Orchids feel the winds of Tibet are still with them."

Zoe gave a little laugh.

"You are so clever," she said. "Only you could think of something like that."

The Duke spread out the fan for her to see, then laid it down again beside the bowl.

Zoe put out her hand and very gently touched the pit in which the Orchid was planted.

To anyone else it might have seemed a casual gesture.

76

But the Duke knew it was how the people of certain countries touch an idol in the Temple or a holy shrine by the road, and say a prayer as they do so.

It told him that Zoe was from a country that was religious.

It was one more item to add to his knowledge of her, which was still so scanty.

He deliberately did not say anything.

As she turned and walked back past the other Orchids, pausing to look first at one and then another, he was sure she was still praying.

He wondered to which God, and in what religion she had been brought up.

He opened the door of the greenhouse.

Once again they stepped out into the moonlight.

They moved through the shrubbery, and as they reached the lawn, Zoe said:

"I can understand how much you love your Orchids. Everyone has to have something to love."

Without thinking, and because the word love made the Duke remember Lois, he replied cynically:

"And you, of course, are looking for a man to love, or should I say men?"

Even as he spoke he thought it was something he should not have said.

Suddenly Zoe replied in a voice he had never heard her use before.

"I hate men! I hate and loathe them! They are evil and wicked!"

She spoke so violently that the Duke could only stop and stare at her.

Then he said:

"I am a man."

Zoe, who was looking away towards the trees, turned her head.

"I am . . . sorry," she said, "I should not have . . .

spoken like that. Of course I was not ... thinking of ... you. You have been so kind and so ... understanding about the orphans that I did not ... think of ... you as ... a man."

The Duke reflected a little dryly that she was the first woman he had ever met who had not thought of him very much as a man.

Because he was intrigued, he put his hand under her arm.

He led her across the grass to where there was a seat under a large chestnut tree.

It was beside the cascading water flowing down through the Garden to the lake.

There was only a faint sound of the Orchestra playing in the distance.

Otherwise everything was very quiet.

As she sat down on the seat, Zoe clasped her hands together.

"Forgive ... me," she said, "I should ... not have ... spoken like ... that."

"You said what was in your heart," the Duke replied, "and now I want to know why you hate men."

There was silence.

He knew she was aware she had made a mistake and was therefore not going to tell him the truth.

She had undoubtedly remembered men who had insulted or upset her.

Yet she was determined to keep acting the part of having been completely concussed.

"I want to ... think just of ... your Orchids," Zoe said.

"You said, and quite rightly," the Duke reminded her, "that everyone has to have something to love. And you are right, I do love my Orchids. What do you love?"

Again there was a silence before Zoe said:

"The children are very . . . sweet and I . . . find it so . . . sad that they have . . . no Father or Mother of . . . their own."

"So you love them," the Duke said.

"They love . . . me," Zoe answered. "When they are frightened or feel . . . lonely at night they creep into bed with . . . me. I . . . hold them . . . close and I . . . think they . . . pretend that I am their . . . Mother."

The Duke thought the way she spoke was very touching.

Aloud he said:

"One day you will have children of your own."

"No! No!" Zoe cried.

The same note of fear was back in her voice.

The Duke knew it was with a tremendous effort of will that she managed to control herself and to add quietly.

"I am very . . . happy in the . . . Orphanage."

"Do you really think, looking as you do, you would want to spend the rest of your life there?"

The Duke was aware it was a question she had asked herself.

He was sure he could read her thoughts as she strove to find an answer which would be the truth but at the same time not revealing.

After several seconds had passed she said:

"There is a . . . great . . . deal . . . to do with the children. Some of them are . . . very talented. A little Italian boy has a . . . beautiful voice."

The Duke made no comment, and she went on:

"Mrs. Winstead and I are wondering if we could organize a concert in which the children could . . . perform and which would . . . entertain the . . . village."

"Of course you must do that," the Duke agreed,

"and it can take place in my private theatre."

"You have your own theatre like . . . ?"

Zoe had made another slip.

The Duke wondered with whom she had been about to compare him as the owner of a theatre.

How was this possible for a girl found alone and penniless on Mount Ararat?

Surely she could never have known anyone rich enough to have a theatre of their own.

"I will show it to you tomorrow," the Duke said, "and I am sure you will think it very suitable for your actors and actresses."

Zoe laughed.

"That is giving them a very grand name, but Mrs. Winstead will be delighted. The villagers have been so kind in so many ways, and she wants the children to thank them and thought this would be a good way of doing so."

"I think it is an excellent idea," the Duke agreed. "I hope you will take part. I would like to see you on stage."

"No . . . of course I could . . . not do . . . that," Zoe said quickly.

"Why not?" the Duke asked.

She did not answer.

He knew here again was another scrap of information, another hint he could add to what he was learning about her.

It was as if he were back in the *Great Game*, trying to find out secrets that had been kept from him.

He must be alert to every word, every intonation, every movement.

Added together they would give him the answer.

He knew that since her arrival for Dinner he had

already learnt a good deal more about her than he had expected.

Something had happened in her life which had made her hate men, something which perhaps had driven her to risk going to Mount Ararat when it was either erupting or on the point of doing so.

Whatever her life had been previously, she had moved, the Duke was sure, in a Social circle which equalled his own.

He had watched her at Dinner when the complicated courses had followed one after the other.

She had never hesitated for a moment as to which knife and fork to use.

Nor had she accepted the wine which had been served with each course.

Anyone who was completely ignorant of how an elaborate Dinner was served would have allowed their wine-glasses to be filled.

Only later would they decide they did not want to drink what was in them.

But when the wines had been brought to Zoe, she just raised her hand to prevent the footman from pouring it into her glass.

The Duke had heard her say:

"May I have some water, please?"

He made no comment but watched her very carefully from the moment she went into the Dining-Room until the moment she came out.

She never did or said anything to suggest that this was a new experience for her.

Now he had learned that she was aware that it was possible for Royalty or a Nobleman to have a private theatre.

That was something he had not expected.

Yet if her background had been a Social one, or if

she came from a responsible family, surely they would be looking for her?

Then he remembered the black veil she had worn over her hair.

He had thought that, as Mrs. Winstead had suggested, it was her shyness.

Now he guessed she was in hiding, but from whom and why?

When the Duke was in the *Great Game* he had learned not only to analyse every word people spoke and everything they did, but to be aware of their vibrations.

He knew now that Zoe was nervous.

She had betrayed herself when he had spoken to her of men.

She was wondering now how to find a plausible explanation.

She wanted to prevent him from questioning, if only in his mind, what she had meant.

Quietly, in a voice that was almost impersonal, the Duke said:

"You are intelligent enough, Zoe, to realise that you are very beautiful. You cannot go through life hiding yourself away as you are trying to do now."

"When they found me on Mount Ararat," Zoe replied, "and took me to Mrs. Winstead, there was no alternative but to come with the children to England. How could I go back to Dogubayazit when I had no money and no idea who I was?"

"Of course to come to England was the sensible thing to do," the Duke said. "I am very grateful both to you and the Gods who sent you to solve my problem."

Almost as if she had forgotten why she was there, Zoe said:

"I am sure your relations want to ask a lot of questions about me, and it would be best if I went back now to the Orphanage."

"That would upset everything," the Duke objected. "I want you to stay here tomorrow, and I feel sure you will be comfortable and enjoy yourself."

"I will do . . . that," Zoe said. "At the same time, I am very . . . afraid of saying . . . the wrong thing or . . . doing something which . . . will make you . . . angry."

"I will not be angry," the Duke promised, "and I am sure, now you have come to Stalbridge Hall, you would like to see my pictures and all the other treasures that have been collected down the ages."

"Yes, I would," Zoe said, "and I would also like, if it is . . . possible, to see . . . your horses."

The Duke looked at her.

"You want to ride?" he enquired.

Zoe made a little sound which he knew was one of excitement.

"Is it possible? You must tell me if I have no . . . right to . . . ask for . . . such a thing. But they talked about your . . . horses in . . . the village and I would be . . . thrilled if I could . . . ride one."

"Then that is what you must do," the Duke said.

"Let me . . . remind you again," Zoe said, "I have . . . nothing . . . to wear, and I would . . . look very . . . strange in what . . . I have on . . . now."

The Duke laughed.

"Even the stable-boys would think you were Diana, Goddess of the Chase," he said. "But I am quite certain Mrs. Partridge can conjure up something. She has never failed in the past to provide anything that is needed, however unusual."

"Then I can ride with you," Zoe said.

Once again the Duke could read her thoughts.

He knew she had not said that as any other woman would have said it, meaning she wanted to be with him personally.

She believed, rather, he would protect her from the other Guests who might see her and want to talk to her and, worst of all, question her.

He knew exactly that was what she was thinking, and he said quietly:

"If you are not too tired, we can ride tomorrow morning before breakfast. I usually go out alone at seven o'clock."

"That would be the most wonderful thing that has . . . happened to . . . me since—"

Once again she stopped.

The Duke knew she had inadvertently given him yet another clue towards the picture he was building up.

He had learned in the *Great Game* not to hurry and not to be impatient.

That was where he knew so many men made a mistake.

Patience was not only a virtue, but one of the hardest to practise.

It was what any man who was analysing another had to learn.

Reluctantly, because he wanted to go on talking to Zoe, the Duke knew that they must go back to the Party.

If they just disappeared or were away too long, there would be sniggers and innuendos, perhaps even some coarse jokes which was not what he wanted in any way connected with Zoe.

When he rose to his feet, she got up too, and without any explanation he led the way back towards the house.

Just before they reached it the Duke avoided the open windows of the Ball-Room and went to a side-door.

It was in fact the one he had used on Thursday night when he had gone to look at the Orchid from Tibet and brought it back with him for Lois.

Now he opened the door and said to Zoe:

"Go to bed now and meet me in the Stables at seven o'clock unless you oversleep."

"I shall not do that," Zoe answered.

"There will be a maid waiting up for you," the Duke said, "Ask her to tell Mrs. Partridge you wish to go riding early and she will understand."

"Thank you," Zoe said. "It is the most exciting thing that has happened to me for a very long time."

She thought the Duke looked at her sharply, and she said quickly:

"What I really . . . mean is that . . . it is the most . . . exciting thing . . . since I was . . . told I was . . . coming to England with . . . the children."

That, the Duke knew, was an afterthought.

He wondered if he would ever learn what was really the last exciting thing that had happened to her.

As she turned in the doorway to say "good-night" to him, the moonlight shone directly on her.

It turned her hair to silver.

Her white dress seemed to shimmer as the Orchids moved when they felt the wind from the fans sweeping through them.

"Good-night, Zoe," the Duke said, "and thank you for all you have done for me."

"Good-night, Your Grace," Zoe replied. "I am so grateful that . . . my prayers were . . . answered and I did not . . . make too . . . many mistakes."

She put out her hand as she spoke and dropped a little curtsy.

As the Duke's fingers closed over hers, he looked into her eyes.

They seemed to have the light of the stars in them.

He suddenly felt that he would like to kiss her.

He was surprised at having such an urge, and at the same time annoyed by it.

After the way Lois had behaved, he had told himself he had finished with women.

Just as Zoe had said she hated men, so he hated Lois and all the young women like her.

But Zoe was different.

Or was she?

The question passed through the Duke's mind.

He told himself that never again would he be deceived.

He took his hand from Zoe's and said:

"Good-night. I hope you sleep well."

He walked away without looking back, and for a moment Zoe stood in the doorway, watching him.

Then she shut the door and ran up the stairs.

As she found her way to her bedroom, she was thinking with excitement that tomorrow she could go riding.

Once again she would be on a horse.

That was something she had missed so acutely that it was hard to put it into words.

Back indoors, the Duke found his relatives staring at him, which made it all too obvious what they were thinking.

He moved through those who were dancing to his Grandmother.

She was seated at the far end of the room, where there were a few comfortable chairs.

"What have you done with that pretty young woman, Ivor?" she asked. "I want to talk to her."

"You will do that tomorrow, Grandmama," the Duke answered. "She is tired and has gone to bed."

"Why did you not tell me about her before?" the Dowager asked. "And how is it possible she cannot remember anything before she was concussed on the mountain?"

"That is exactly what is puzzling the Doctors," the Duke replied.

"Sad, very sad," the Dowager Duchess murmured. "But you must tell me how you met her, and is it really true you intend to marry her?"

"We will talk about it tomorrow, Grandmama," the Duke replied. "It is getting late, and I think, after such a long day and so much excitement over the Point-to-Point, most people will be ready to retire to bed."

"You are right, dear boy," the Dowager said. "It really is long past my bedtime."

The Duke helped her to her feet and led her to the bottom of the stairs, where her lady's-maid was waiting for her.

He kissed her good-night.

Then he went back to the Ball-Room to tell the orchestra to play "God Save the Queen."

"Oh, must we stop, Cousin Ivor?" some of his younger Cousins pleaded.

"I will give a real Ball for you some time later in the year," the Duke promised. "But now we have all had a long day and I expect most of you will be travelling tomorrow."

"I suppose so," several of them said reluctantly.

To his consternation, one or two of the older members of his family said:

"We would like to stay on until Monday or Tuesday, Ivor. There is a lot we want to talk to you about."

The Duke was certain this concerned his marriage, and in the meantime he hurried his relatives upstairs.

Finally, when those who were staying in other houses had gone, the front door was shut and locked.

The Duke went into his Study to pick up some papers he wanted to read upstairs, and Charles came in.

He was alone, and the Duke, shutting the drawer of his desk, said:

"I suppose, Charles, the Minfordburys are leaving tomorrow morning."

"As early as possible," Charles replied, "and they do not wish to see you before they go."

The Duke knew this was a relief.

Then Charles said in a different tone:

"Do you want me to go too?"

The Duke shook his head.

"No," he said quickly.

Charles hesitated a moment, then in a somewhat embarrassed voice he said:

"I have no idea how you became aware of what was going on, but I want you to know that it was not after you met Lois, but some time before, that she and I meant anything to each other."

The Duke walked towards the door.

"I do not want to discuss it, Charles," he said. "It was a mistake, and the sooner we both forget it the better. But let me assure you once and for all that I have no intention of ever getting married."

He left the room as he finished speaking.

Charles heard him going down the corridor towards the Hall.

It had passed off better than he had feared, and he was deeply grateful he would not lose the Duke's friendship.

He was not thinking of all the advantages that friendship had brought him.

They were really immaterial.

But he had always felt as if Ivor were his brother, and he knew that if he were shut out of his life, nothing could ever replace that friendship.

The mistake he had made was in thinking that by helping the Duke to get married to Lois he was doing him a good turn.

"I have made a mess of this," Charles told himself miserably. "But then, have I ever done anything else?"

He went upstairs realising he was the last Guest to do so.

He went into his bedroom and shut the door.

He knew he would not go to Lois tonight or any other night.

Like the Duke, he had made a mistake, and the sooner they both forgot about it, the better.

The Duke, to his surprise, slept well and woke at six-thirty.

He had trained himself when he was in the Army to wake at the hour he wanted without needing his Batman to call him.

Even as he got out of bed, Hubert came into the room carrying his riding-boots.

"Good-morning, Your Grace," he said. "It is a fine morning and I understands Miss Zoe'll be waiting for you at th' Stables."

The Duke knew this meant that Mrs. Partridge had got the message he had told Zoe to send her.

He disliked talking first thing in the morning, and washed and clothed himself in silence.

Only as Hubert handed him his gloves and whip did he say:

"I thought Your Grace'd like to know that th' Marquess and Marchioness of Minfordbury are leaving at eight o'clock with Lady Lois."

The Duke thought this certainly cleared the decks.

He hurried downstairs and out by the door at the back of the house which led to the Stables.

When he got there, he found Zoe was already mounted on one of his finest horses.

It was a well-bred but strong-willed and obstreperous animal.

He was convinced she had chosen it against the advice of his Head Groom.

He only hoped she was not over-estimating her riding ability.

She appeared to be sitting comfortably in the saddle and quite unperturbed by the restlessness of the horse beneath her.

The Duke's Stallion was ready for him and he swung himself into the saddle.

He followed Zoe, who was already at the far end of the yard, where there was a gate opening onto one of the paddocks.

As he joined her, he said:

"Good-morning, Zoe. I see you have chosen one of the more difficult horses in my Stable."

Zoe smiled at him.

"I felt that was what I wanted this morning. Your groom was very insistent that I will end up in a ditch."

"I hope not," the Duke replied. "It will certainly spoil our ride if I have to carry you home."

"You need not worry," Zoe answered. "The only thing I might do is to fall off from sheer excitement."

The Duke looked at her.

He realised that Mrs. Partridge had once more produced exactly what was necessary.

He guessed that Zoe was wearing a habit which had belonged to his Mother.

It fitted her quite well, only being a little loose round the waist.

He noticed that her hair, as was correct, was pinned very closely to her head.

The hat she wore over it might be somewhat out of date but was certainly very becoming.

It had, in fact, as he was well aware, been the fashion some years ago.

It was introduced by the women who met at the statue of Achilles in Hyde Park and rode in Rotten Row.

They were know as the "Pretty Horsebreakers."

They were not, as many people supposed, prostitutes on horseback.

They were exceptionally skilled riders who broke in the horses offered for sale in London.

It was, however, possible for a man to purchase one of these horses, and for the rider to be included in the deal.

The Pretty Horsebreakers had looked enchanting in this particular form of headwear.

It had a high crown surrounded by a floating gauze veil.

After two or three years it was copied by the ladies of the Beau Monde.

The Duke's Mother must have succumbed to the temptation to look so attractive on horseback, or perhaps it was just a hat that had been left behind by a visitor.

At any rate, it made Zoe look very lovely.

At the same time, it was firm on her head and not likely to fall off as she took her horse over a jump.

They set off over the flat land at a good gallop.

Then when they settled down to move a little more slowly, the Duke said teasingly:

"How could I have imagined a girl from an Orphanage would be an experienced horsewoman?"

"How could I imagine, coming from an Orphanage, I would be offered such a magnificent horse to ride?" Zoe parried.

"You handle him better than anyone else has managed to do," the Duke said. "I am interested to know why you deliberately chose what is undoubtedly the most difficult horse in my Stable."

"I felt like fighting a battle this morning," Zoe replied, "and therefore *Sultan* had to be my opponent."

"I am sure he appreciates his importance," the Duke said slightly sarcastically.

Zoe looked at him.

"Are you . . . telling me," she asked in a rather small voice, "that I am . . . taking . . . advantage of my . . . position and being what . . . your young Cousins . . . would call pushy?"

The Duke laughed.

"How did you know that was the sort of slang they used?" he enquired.

"I heard them last night at Dinner," Zoe said, "and realised from what they were saying that I am very much out of date."

The Duke laughed again.

"Nobody who looked at you sitting beside me last night would accuse you of that."

"You are so . . . clever," Zoe said in a low voice. "You make me feel . . . very . . . foolish."

92

"That is the last thing of which I would accuse you," the Duke said.

He wondered if he should add that he thought she was in fact extremely clever and that he was sure she was in hiding, and pretending very cleverly that she was still suffering from concussion.

Then he thought it was too soon.

He had no wish to frighten her.

He realised that quite on her own she was walking a tightrope.

Any other young woman of the same age would be terrified.

Wherever she came from, whoever her parents were, she was now alone in the world without a penny.

She had to rely on the kindness of a man she had never seen until two days ago.

"Surely," the Duke said silently, "she is wondering what the future holds for her?"

If in fact she was hiding from somebody, there must always be for her the fear that she would be discovered.

"I must somehow make her confide in me," he told himself.

At the same time, he was sure it was not going to be easy.

There was a reserve about Zoe that he had not found in other women, especially where he was concerned.

There was also, he thought, a pride and self-control which must come from good breeding.

"Who is she? Who can she possibly be?" he was asking himself as they rode side by side. "And how can I help her if she will not tell me the truth, if she will not trust me?"

It suddenly seemed to the Duke to be of tremendous importance to him that Zoe should trust him.

He would have to exert his charm, which had never failed him in the past.

He felt it was the most intriguing investigation he had ever undertaken.

It was certainly one in which he started with no assistance, no guidelines.

Most extraordinary of all, he had not the slightest idea what he would find at the end of his journey towards the truth.

It was exactly the sort of exercise the Duke knew he needed at that moment.

If Zoe had not been there, he would have been feeling resentful, frustrated, and humiliated by Lois.

As it was, already he could tell himself quite truthfully that she had passed out of his life.

Soon he would literally never think of her again.

Instead, the problem of Zoe, and who she could be, was filling his mind.

It would make him more determined hour by hour and day by day to help her if it was possible for him to do so.

chapter five

THE Duke was relieved when he learned the Minfordburys had actually left.

They had obviously not wanted to see him before
they went.

Gradually, as the morning went on, his relations
came downstairs.

Several of the ladies, including his Grandmother,
said they were going to Church.

He wondered if Zoe would go with them too.

Then, using his perception, he realised that if, as he
supposed, she had been to Church with the orphans,
she would have worn the Protestant veil over her
hair, as she could not do now.

He therefore thought it sensible of her not to come
downstairs until after the party going to Church had
left.

She was looking exceedingly lovely in yet another
dress that Miss Lawson had altered for her.

It was very simple.

Miss Lawson had removed a lot of the more elaborate decorations which had been suitable for an older woman.

The Duke was not surprised when he looked for Zoe a little later to find her in the Library.

She was looking through a pile of books she had put on the sofa beside her.

When he came in, she exclaimed:

"What exciting books you have in your Library! There are so many! Have you read them all?"

The Duke laughed.

"Not quite all," he answered, "but of course I have several years left in which I can do so."

"That is one thing I am going to ask you to give the Orphanage," Zoe said.

"You mean they need a Library," the Duke answered. "That should not be difficult."

"It is so important," Zoe said seriously, "that children should learn to read when they are young and enjoy it. It is the quickest and best way of educating oneself, but few people seem to realise that."

The Duke thought she was talking like an old woman rather than a young girl, and he asked:

"Why do books mean so much to you?"

"Because they teach one about life," Zoe answered.

"Do you think they taught you a lot," the Duke asked, "before you were concussed?"

He realised that he had caught her out again.

She had been talking as if she had read books, and a great many of them, in the years which she was supposed to have forgotten.

If, however, Zoe realised what he was implying, she showed no sign of it.

"This book," she said, "is all about India, and I am sure you must have read it before you went there. I find the pictures fascinating.''

The Duke knew the book to which she referred, and said:

"One day you must visit India. I think you will find it different from what you expect. It certainly opens new horizons in the mind.''

"That is what I am looking for,'' Zoe said quietly, as if she were speaking to herself.

"There is another book here,'' the Duke said, "which I know you will enjoy.''

He went to one of the shelves on the other side of the room.

As he did so, the door opened and a man Zoe had not seen before came into the room.

"Good morning, Ivor,'' the newcomer said.

The Duke looked round, surprised, and said:

"Lionel! Where have you sprung from?''

"I came down from London yesterday,'' was the reply, "and was told you had a huge party here of your relatives, but I had been omitted.''

The Duke smiled and, walking towards him, held out his hand.

"I never thought to ask you,'' he said, "because you do not as a rule seem one of the family.''

"Nevertheless, I am one, and I am very piqued at not being invited to such an important family occasion.''

As the newcomer finished speaking, he looked very obviously towards Zoe.

As if the Duke understood, he said:

"Let me introduce you, Zoe. This is Lord Redford, who is a distant Cousin of mine.''

Lord Redford walked towards the sofa on which Zoe was sitting.

She held out her hand and Lord Redford took it in both his.

"Now I understand," he said, "why, as they have all been telling me, you have bowled them over. They had never met you before, but now they will find you impossible to forget."

The way Lord Redford spoke, still holding Zoe's hand tightly in his and looking at her with admiration in his eyes, made her shy.

The Duke saw the colour come into her cheeks.

She looked away from Lord Redford, attempting to take her hand from his.

"Only you, Ivor," Lord Redford went on, "could find anyone so exquisite who at the same time has, I understand, an intriguing and thought-provoking background."

"I expect you have been told," the Duke answered in a cold voice, "that Zoe was injured at the recent eruption of Mount Ararat and has not yet recovered her memory."

"I was also told she was breathlessly beautiful," Lord Redford said, "and that I find very true."

Now, with an effort, Zoe extricated her hand.

She moved quickly from where she had been sandwiched between the sofa and Lord Redford and said to the Duke:

"I have some things to see to . . . upstairs."

Moving swiftly across the room, she reached the door before he could open it for her and vanished.

"Let me congratulate you, Ivor," Lord Redford said. "Only you could have been clever enough to find anyone so beautiful, and surprise all the old trouts who thought you were going to marry Lois Minford."

The Duke had no wish to talk about his private affairs.

Somewhat obviously he said:

"You have not told me what you are doing in this part of the World. You are usually too engaged in London to come to the country."

He had never liked this distant Cousin of his, and he had avoided him whenever it was possible.

He was well aware that Lionel Redford wanted to ingratiate himself.

It was because he wanted to be asked to the Parties the Duke gave in London and to those very much sought after which he gave in the country.

Lionel Redford had always been somewhat of a "black sheep" where his relations were concerned.

His Father had left him a certain amount of money beside the title.

He had never troubled to find himself anything intelligent to do.

He spent his time with the young men who haunted the stage-doors of Drury Lane and other theatres.

He gambled at Whites and other Clubs.

He had a series of *affaires de coeur* with women who were gossiped about.

In fact, the Duke rather despised Lionel Redford, thinking that at the age of twenty-eight he was wasting his life.

He was still what the older people called "sowing his wild oats" as if he were a young man of eighteen.

"Now, come on, Ivor, don't be snooty," Lord Redford said, throwing himself down comfortably on the sofa. "Tell me where you found this pretty little pigeon who has obviously just come out of the egg, and if you really intend to marry her."

99

Only the Duke's iron self-control saved him from telling Lord Redford to mind his own business.

Instead, he said:

"I expect, Lionel, you would like a drink, and do you intend to stay for Luncheon?"

"I should be extremely upset if you turned me away just as the meal is announced," Lord Redford replied, "and of course I must have a glass of Champagne to drink your health."

"That will be waiting for us in another room," the Duke said.

Without waiting for Lord Redford to rise, he walked ahead down the passage.

He was thinking how unfortunate it was that his most unwanted Cousin should turn up at this moment.

The one thing he did not want was a great deal of gossip about Zoe in London.

There was no doubt that every tit-bit Lionel could pick up would be taken straight back to Whites Club.

In the room where they usually met before Luncheon, the Duke found his Grandmother and his other relations.

"Oh, here you are, Ivor," one of them exclaimed. "We thought we had lost you."

"I am still here," the Duke replied, "and we have a new visitor who was not expected."

As he spoke, Lord Redford came into the room behind him.

The Duke could not help noticing with a twist of his lips the expression on the faces of his relatives.

It was not one of dislike, but something not far from it.

Lord Redford, however, was quite unabashed.

He kissed the ladies, shook the hands of the men,

100

and told them how delighted he was to be there.

"I cannot imagine," he said, "why I was forgotten last night! I could not drink Ivor's health then, but better late than never!"

He raised the glass of Champagne which he held in his hand and said:

"To Ivor, and may he never topple off his pedestal."

It was a toast that most of the party did not think very funny.

Only two of the younger men winked at each other.

"What are you doing these days, Lionel?" the Dowager Duchess asked.

"Enjoying myself," Lord Redford replied. "And of course looking for someone pretty and witty to amuse me."

He spoke almost defiantly, as if he had no intention of being humiliated by any criticism.

Two more of the Duke's relatives came into the room and were surprised to see Lord Redford.

They, like the rest, were told how disappointed he was that he had not been invited the previous evening.

The Duke glanced at the clock.

There were only two minutes to pass before Luncheon would be announced.

He wondered what had happened to Zoe.

As if by thinking of her he had summoned her, she came into the room a minute later.

She moved swiftly towards the Dowager Duchess's chair and knelt down beside it.

"I hope you are not too tired, Ma'am, after last night," she said in her soft voice.

"I enjoyed every minute of it," the Duchess answered, "but I was rather surprised that you did not dance to that delightful band."

"I did dance a Waltz with the Duke," Zoe said, "and then, after we had put his beautiful Orchid back in the greenhouse, I went to bed."

"So that is what you were doing," the Duchess said in a tone of satisfaction. "I think it was very sensible of you not to stay up too late."

Zoe smiled at her.

She looked so pretty as she did so that the Duke could understand why his Grandmother reached out and touched Zoe affectionately on the shoulder.

"Help me out of my chair, dear child," she said. "I know my grandson dislikes people taking too long to reach the Dining-Room."

Zoe helped her to her feet just as Dawson announced Luncheon.

The Duke had arranged the seating much the same as it had been the night before.

His Grandmother was on his right and Zoe on his left.

He left most of the family to choose where they wished to sit.

He managed, by thinking quickly, to put one of his Uncles next to Zoe, just in time to prevent Lord Redford from taking that seat.

He knew that Zoe would be embarrassed and perhaps rather frightened by the uninhibited compliments he knew Lionel would pay her.

As they sat down, he thought again it was a great pity that he had arrived uninvited at Stalbridge Hall.

Luncheon, however, passed off with everyone talking about the Point-to-Point.

Quite a spirited discussion took place as to which horse should actually have won the jumping competition.

Then an elderly couple informed the Duke they were leaving straight away and he went with them to the hall to see them into their carriage.

There was, however, some delay.

His Cousin found she had left a chiffon veil she wore over her hat upstairs.

A footman was sent to find it.

While they were waiting, the rest of the party having said "good-bye," moved away.

The footman came back to report that the veil could not be found, and Mrs. Partridge said that everything in Her Ladyship's room had been packed in her luggage.

The Duke's Cousin refused to start off on the journey home in an open carriage without tying her hat firmly on her head.

This meant that one of the cases which had been placed on the back of the carriage had to be unpacked.

It took two footmen to get out the right case, to unstrap it, and find what Her Ladyship required.

Finally the chiffon veil was discovered.

Its owner draped it over the top of her hat and tied it in a bow under her chin.

The case was put back where it had been before.

There was nothing the Duke could do but wait as patiently as he could until they finally drove away.

With a sigh of relief he saw them moving swiftly down the long drive.

As he turned and walked back up the steps into the hall, he wondered what had happened in his absence and if Zoe was all right.

He went first into the room where they had gathered before Luncheon was announced.

His Grandmother was there and most of the relatives who were still staying in the house.

There was, however, no sign of Zoe or of Lord Redford.

The Duke had hoped that when they left the Dining-Room, Zoe would have the sense to stay with his Grandmother and the rest of the party.

It was, in fact, what she had intended to do.

Then, when the Duke was held up outside the front door, she saw by the expression in Lord Redford's eyes as he came into the room that he intended to talk to her.

Fortunately he was diverted from coming immediately to her side by the Duke's Uncle asking him if he would like a liqueur.

Coffee had already been served in the Dining-Room.

Most of the men had a glass of port at the same time.

Liqueurs had now been brought into the other room with small glasses from which to drink them.

Lionel Redford replied that he would like a Brandy.

As it was being poured into a glass for him, Zoe slipped away.

She moved quickly and with the same grace that the Duke had noticed before Dinner the night before.

She disappeared before anyone realised what was happening.

She slipped down the corridor and went into the room at the end of it which was known as "The Blue Room."

This was because the curtains were blue and so were the cushions on the comfortable sofa chairs.

She wanted to visit it because it contained a number of exquisite miniatures.

They had been collected over the centuries.

While the majority were of Dukes and Duchesses

of Stalbridge, there were also miniatures of Royal Families of all nationalities of each age.

There were two particularly beautiful French miniatures of Queen Marie Antoinette, and several, decorated with jewels, which depicted Russian Tsars and Tsarinas.

Zoe had had only a very quick glance at this room previously.

Now she thought, as she shut the door, that she would enjoy looking at the miniatures more closely and trying to recognise who they were.

She was holding in her hand an excellent likeness of Charles II when the door opened.

To her consternation, Lord Redford came in.

"Why did you disappear?" he asked. "You must have known quite well I want to talk to you."

"And I want to study these miniatures," Zoe replied.

"Do you find them so very interesting," Lord Redford enquired, "when they have all been dead for the last hundred years?"

Zoe did not answer, and he went nearer to her, saying:

"You and I are very much alike and that, believe me, is far more exciting."

He was now standing just behind her, and Zoe suddenly felt frightened.

She was alone in a room at the far end of the corridor.

Lord Redford was taller than the average man.

It was impossible not to be aware of the forcefulness of his personality.

He imposed himself on people for whatever he wished to do.

He was still standing just behind her.

Zoe felt as if he were drawing her closer and closer to him so that she could not escape.

A little incoherently, she said:

"The Dowager Duchess . . . wants . . . me."

"I can assure you," Lord Redford said, moving round to face her, "that she does not want you as much as I do. I find you entrancing, Zoe. I want to talk to you and to tell you how different you are from anyone I have ever seen before."

"I am sure that is . . . not true," Zoe said. "Please, I want to . . . go back to the . . . other . . . room."

"You cannot expect me to let you leave me, when we are so fortunate as to be here alone without those fuddy-duddies chattering beside us."

"You should . . . not be so . . . rude about . . . your relations," Zoe managed to say a little aggressively.

Lionel Redford laughed.

"It is nothing to what they say about me! There is no love whatsoever lost between us. But talking of love, that is a subject for you and me."

"I cannot think why you should say . . . such things . . . to me," Zoe retorted, "when I have only . . . just met . . . you."

"I am saying them because I was astonished when I first saw you, and even more astonished when I look at you now," Lord Redford declared. "You are very beautiful, and when you come to London every man there will be at your feet."

"That is . . . something I do not . . . want," Zoe said, "and anyway I am . . . not coming . . . to London."

"You are staying here with my Cousin Ivor?" Lord Redford questioned. "I think you'll find it rather dull after a while. I will show you how amusing and delightful London can be if one knows the right way to go about it."

While he was talking, Lord Redford moved a little nearer to Zoe.

She was trapped between the wall with the miniatures on it and a narrow table below them.

On this there were still more miniatures.

She wondered desperately how she could get away.

As she glanced quickly from side to side, he was watching her.

"Why should you want to escape," he asked, "when the excitement of our first meeting is with us? All I want to tell you is how utterly desirable you are. Surely that is something you want to hear?"

"No!" Zoe said quickly. "I want to . . . find His . . . Grace, so please . . . let me pass."

"And if I do not, what will you do about it?" Lord Redford asked.

There was a glint in his eye.

It would have told anyone who knew him that this was the type of encounter he most enjoyed.

As far as he was concerned, the end was inevitable.

He had always found it impossible to resist a new and pretty girl he had not met before.

Zoe was exceptional.

He was determined to keep her within his grasp, and not let her escape.

"You fascinate me," he said. "How is it possible that my greatly admired and so very proud of himself Cousin could have found you before anyone else did?"

"I am . . . sure he will be . . . only too . . . pleased to . . . tell you . . . himself how it . . . happened," Zoe said a little breathlessly.

"But I would rather you tell me," Lord Redford replied, "and with your lips close to mine I will listen to every word."

He tried to put his arm around Zoe, and she gave a little scream of fright.

Even as she did so, the door opened and the Duke came in.

He saw what was happening at a glance.

As he moved towards them, Zoe pushed past Lord Redford although he tried to stop her and ran towards the Duke.

"What are you doing here?" the Duke asked sharply.

"I came . . . to look . . . at the miniatures," Zoe murmured.

Her eyes looking up at the Duke's were frightened in the same way that he had seen them before.

"Go and put on your hat," he said. "I will take you to the Orphanage as we arranged."

The sunshine was back in Zoe's eyes.

She gave him a quick glance which said a great deal more than words before she ran to the door.

Lord Redford turned round.

"Trust you, Ivor," he said, "always to come in at the wrong moment."

The Duke looked him up and down before he said coldly:

"You should keep your conversation and your attentions for actresses and prostitutes. They may enjoy it, but not the young women you are likely to meet in this house."

"You deceive yourself," Lord Redford retorted. "They may tell you one thing, but I assure you all women like it, and the more bawdy the better."

With difficulty the Duke controlled his temper.

"That is what you may believe, but some women are different," he said quietly. "I think, Lionel, you should go back to your native haunts, where you are better appreciated."

He was being mockingly sarcastic, but Lord Redford merely laughed.

"When you get a little older, my dear Cousin," he said, "you will learn that not only are all cats grey in the dark, but however easily they may deceive you, they are all after the same thing, and that is—a man."

He did not wait for the Duke's reply, but walked out of "The Blue Room."

He went back down the corridor to where the rest of his family were still talking.

For a moment the Duke did not follow him.

He knew very well that Lionel was blustering it out in his usual fashion.

The way he was behaving did not really surprise him.

He had done so for the last eight years, and everyone treated it more or less as a joke.

Yet he was quite certain that Zoe had been really frightened when he came into the room.

If he had been only a little later he would have found her struggling against Lord Redford as he tried to kiss her.

Then he asked himself if that was true.

Would she really have struggled?

Would she have fought to get away?

Or was she another Lois merely acting the part of a young and innocent girl?

Could he be blinded and decieved for a second time?

Had the scream he had heard as he opened the door been one of genuine fear?

Zoe had said emphatically—almost as though she could not stop herself—that she hated men.

Was that true?

Or was Lionel telling the truth when he said all women liked it?

For a moment the Duke queried his own convictions.

He asked himself if he could really believe in Zoe.

He was quite convinced that if she had lost her memory on Mount Ararat, it was restored by now.

At the same time, he believed her when she said she hated men.

She had been genuinely frightened just now when Lord Redford was obviously trying to hold her by force.

As the Duke walked down the corridor, he told himself he would find out the truth if it was the last thing he ever did.

It was not possible that after a career of acclaimed successes, he should now have a failure.

Zoe had gone upstairs as the Duke had told her to do.

She collected her hat and just a chiffon scarf to put over her shoulders.

When they had been out riding and were moving slowly through a wood, she said:

"I have just remembered it is the birthday today of a little Italian boy who I told you has such a good singing voice. Would it be asking too much if I could take him . . . something this . . . afternoon?"

"Of course," the Duke replied. "I will tell the Chef to ice a cake. I remember that is what I enjoyed at that age."

"Oh, thank you . . . thank you," Zoe cried, "you are . . . so kind."

When they got back to the house, before she went upstairs to her bedroom, the Duke said:

"I will order the cake for your birthday boy, and we will take it over to him this afternoon."

She flashed him a smile of gratitude before she ran upstairs to change, and told herself:

"Only the Duke could be kind enough to think of a child of six and be prepared to take a cake to him."

Now, as she reached her bedroom, she felt herself shiver because she had been so frightened by Lord Redford.

'I hate him as I hate all men,' she thought. 'How could I have been so silly as to think he would not follow me? I should have stayed with the others.'

She had been trembling when she left "The Blue Room."

It was several minutes before her breath came evenly between her lips and she no longer had that strange and frightening feeling in her breast.

She put on her hat.

It was a very pretty one which had belonged to the Duke's Mother but had been redecorated by Miss Lawson with just a few flowers and some velvet ribbon.

When Zoe looked in the mirror, she wondered what Mrs. Winstead would think when she saw her.

Then she wondered further if she dared go into the village without the veil she had always worn over her hair.

But she knew she did not want the Duke to see her like that again.

'If I get out of the carriage quickly at the Orphanage,' she thought, 'and run into the house, no-one will see me except the children and Mrs. Winstead. They do not matter.'

Then she began to wonder how she could go downstairs and find the Duke without perhaps running into Lord Redford again.

There was a knock at the door.

When Zoe opened it, the Duke was standing outside.

"Are you ready?" he asked.

"Yes, of course, but I did not want to come and look for you in case—"

"It is all right," the Duke interrupted. "He is with the rest of the party, and as I have no intention of asking him to stay, he will leave before this evening."

The Duke and Zoe went down the stairs.

Then, as they turned into the corridor which led in the direction of the Stables, he said:

"Were you really frightened just now?"

It was a question Zoe had not expected, and the Duke saw the colour come into her cheeks.

Then in a little voice he could hardly hear, she said:

"I hate him . . . I loathe him . . . please do not . . . let him come . . . near me . . . again."

The Duke was convinced that every word was absolutely sincere.

He thought he could stake his whole fortune that what she said was the truth.

"Do not worry," he answered, "I will deal with it."

They went out to the Stables where the Chaise was waiting for them in the Stable-Yard.

As Zoe got in, one of the Stable-boys came from the house carrying a large plate.

On it there was a cake on which was written in pink and white icing "Happy Birthday."

"Oh! That is wonderful!" Zoe exclaimed. "Antonio will be thrilled!"

"I am afraid you will have to carry it on your lap,"

the Duke said. "We thought of putting it in the back, but if I move quickly, it may topple over."

"Of course I will carry it," Zoe said. "It would be wicked to let it break, when it looks so pretty."

There were also little rosettes of icing all round the cake.

When it had been placed on Zoe's knees, another Stable-boy put a box down beside her feet.

"Them be the candles, Miss," he explained.

As they drove away, she said to the Duke:

"How can you be so clever as to think of everything?"

"You thought of the cake," he answered.

"But not the candles," Zoe replied. "Once again you are waving your magic wand to make someone happy."

It was a compliment, the Duke was sure, which genuinely came from the very depths of her heart.

There was nothing the least flirtatious in the way she said it, nor did she even look at him.

As he drove on, he told himself it was impossible that this was an act.

But it infuriated him that Lord Redford should have made him suspicious.

When they arrived at the Orphanage, the Duke drove up very close to the door.

Zoe was able to slip in without anyone in the street noticing her.

She was carrying the cake in her hands.

The children came running towards her, shouting out her name—"Zoe . . . Zoe!"

One of them asked:

"What have you got there?"

"A cake for Antonio," she answered, "because it is

his birthday. Have you remembered to wish him 'Many happy returns'?"

One or two of the older children nodded and said they had.

"He didn't have any presents," one of them said.

"I know that," Zoe replied, "and this is a present from His Grace and from me. So hurry and lay the table so that Antonio can cut it and make a wish."

"I shall wish we can have a birthday every day," one of the children said.

"You can be born only once, stupid," one of the others pointed out.

They were eagerly watching her put the cake down on the table.

It made Zoe wonder if it would be possible that each of the children should have a cake on their birthday sent down from the Big House, as they called it in the village.

"I am sure if I asked the Duke he would agree," she told herself.

Then she thought of Lord Redford, and a little shiver ran through her.

"I hate him," she told herself again, "as I hate all men—except, of course, the Duke. He is different."

Mrs. Winstead was delighted with the cake and helped to arrange the candles.

Then twenty minutes before their usual tea-time a bell was rung.

The children came running in, scrambled into their seats, and looked excitedly at the cake.

Zoe came in last, as she had been washing Antonio's hands.

As they neared the table, she picked him up in her arms so that he could see the cake better.

"That is your cake, Antonio," she said, speaking in

Italian, "and you have six candles because you are six today."

She sat him down in a chair opposite the cake and explained to him before she helped him to cut the first slice that he must wish for something he wanted very much.

"Now, think, Antonio. What do you want more than anything else in the whole world?"

"I want my . . . Mama," Antonio replied.

Because it was such an unexpected reply, the Duke saw the tears come into Zoe's eyes.

She put her arms round the little boy and held him very close.

Then she put the knife into his hand and made him kneel on his chair so that it was easier for him to cut the cake.

There was a large slice for everyone and a small slice for the Duke.

Zoe managed to keep just enough over for Antonio's supper.

The children gobbled up the cake and said it was delicious.

Then they all toasted Antonio with the milk they were drinking.

He thanked them with a deep bow which Zoe told him to make.

"Now I think we ought to get back," the Duke remarked.

"It has been lovely to have you here," Mrs. Winstead said, "but, oh, I forgot to tell you, Zoe, we had a visitor this morning. Ever such a nice gentleman, he was. He had heard about us coming here all the way from Turkey and was very interested to know how many different nationalities the Orphans represented."

The Duke was hardly listening.

Then he realised that Zoe was looking at Mrs. Winstead with a strange expression on her face.

As she finished speaking, Zoe said in a low voice:

"Did this gentleman . . . ask about . . . me?"

"As a matter of fact, he did," Mrs. Winstead replied. "But I remembered you told me what to say. I told him you left us soon after we arrived in England."

The Duke thought that Zoe seemed to relax.

But he was well aware that while she was waiting to hear Mrs. Winstead's answer, there had been an unmistakable expression of fear in her eyes.

They got into the Chaise.

The horses had been looked after by one of the village boys to whom the Duke gave sixpence.

Then, waving to the children, they set off back towards the Hall.

As they drove down the village street, the Duke saw that Zoe was looking from side to side.

It was as if she were searching for someone among the few villagers to be seen at this time of day.

Only when they turned into the drive did she sit back and seem to relax.

The Duke slowed his horses.

"Why did you tell Mrs. Winstead," he asked, "that if anyone asked where you were after you had come here from Turkey, she was to say you had left the Orphanage?"

Zoe did not answer, and he went on:

"I thought when I came to the Orphanage to ask for help that you had every intention of staying there indefinitely."

There was silence.

Then after a moment he said:

"Tell me why you did that. I am finding it difficult to understand why you are so frightened and of whom."

He knew as they drove on that Zoe was thinking quickly.

At last she said:

"Someone from . . . Turkey might want to . . . take me back to . . . where I was . . . before I lost my memory . . . and I want to stay . . . here."

The Duke thought a little wryly she had extricated herself from an awkward situation very cleverly.

At the same time, she had not told the truth.

Why was she hiding?

Why was she frightened?

Above all, was he being deceived for a second time?

chapter six

Zoe could not sleep, and she twisted and turned in her bed.

However hard she tried, she could not get away from her thoughts.

She was worrying about the man that Mrs. Winstead had said was such a "nice gentleman."

How could he have heard about her coming here from Turkey, and why should he be interested?

The questions kept asking themselves again and again.

Finally the first fingers of dawn showed on either side of the curtains.

By six-thirty she had dressed herself and, wearing her riding-habit, she went to the Stables.

They were surprised to see her so early.

She explained to the groom she was just going into the village before she rode with the Duke.

She would be back at seven o'clock, when his Stallion would be taken round to the front door.

The young groom who had been half asleep when Zoe arrived was not particularly interested in what she had to say.

She rode as quickly as possible down the drive into the village which led to the Orphanage.

Zoe tied her horse up to the fence.

When Mrs. Winstead opened the door, she was astonished to see her.

"Good Heavens!" she exclaimed. "What are you doing here at this hour of the morning?"

"I wanted to see you," Zoe replied.

She walked into the hall, and, shutting the front door, Mrs. Winstead followed her.

"What about?" she asked.

"I am interested in the gentleman who called on you and asked questions about the orphans."

"Oh, him!" Mrs. Winstead said. "I told you he was a very nice gentleman."

"Was he English?" Zoe asked.

There was a pause, and Mrs. Winstead wrinkled her brow.

"I am not quite certain," she replied. "He spoke very good English, but he might have had some other blood in him. It was difficult to tell."

"What did he say," Zoe enquired, "after you told him I had left you?"

"He asked if I knew where you had gone, and I said I had not heard from you for some time."

Zoe did not speak, and after a moment Mrs. Winstead said:

"I don't know why you are worrying about it any more than I know why you asked me to lie about you. After all, there is nothing wrong in losing your memory."

"No, of course not," Zoe agreed, "and thank you very much for doing as I asked you."

As she spoke, one of the little orphans ran into the room.

"Billy has cut his finger," she told Mrs. Winstead, "and it's bleeding."

"Oh, bother!" said Mrs. Winstead. "That is the second time that child has cut himself, and I haven't got a bandage left in the house."

"I am going back now," Zoe said. "Shall I ask Mr. Geary at the shop to send you some bandages?"

"Yes, do, dear," Mrs. Winstead said. "That will be very kind. I'd better have a dozen or so. The children are always cutting themselves."

Zoe left the Orphanage and, mounting her horse, rode down the street.

Mr. Geary's shop was at the far end and provided everything that anyone could possibly want.

His large bow window had a remarkable variety of articles for sale.

There was fresh bread which Mrs. Geary baked in their kitchen, and the sweets which the children loved to suck, which was only when they were fortunate enough to have a penny in their possession.

It was still very early and the door was closed.

Zoe dismounted and tied her horse, which fortunately was a quiet one, to a gate-post.

As she walked towards the door, it was thrown open.

Mr. Geary was sweeping out his shop.

He had sprinkled the floor with water and with a hard brush was sweeping out the dirt and the dust.

Anything lying on the floor was swept out onto the pavement and into the gutter.

To avoid getting her riding-boots wet, Zoe managed deftly to step through the doorway and get to the counter.

"You're early, Miss," Mr. Geary said. "I won't be a minute getting this rubbish outside."

As he spoke, he swept up a crumpled paper bag and some pieces of a stale bun.

Then, as he brushed them all with a splash into the gutter, a Chaise drew up outside.

There were four men in it.

The one who was driving the two horses pulling it shouted:

"Which—the way to—the Orphanage?"

Mr. Geary straightened himself.

"You go straight up the road," he said, "and it be the last house on the right-hand side."

As he was speaking, Zoe peeped through the window at the newcomers.

When she saw who was sitting in the front of the Chaise, she stiffened, and her hand went to her breast.

Then, as they drove away, she rushed out of the shop, saying to Mr. Geary as she passed him:

"Please send Mrs. Winstead twelve bandages."

"Twelve bandages," Mr. Geary repeated. "What size? You're in a terrible hurry, Miss Zoe."

To his amazement, Zoe did not stop to listen.

She was already urging her horse forward and hurrying towards the great gates which led up to the Hall.

Once she was in the drive, she galloped as fast as she could on the soft grass.

As the house came into sight and then the courtyard in front of it, she saw the Duke's Stallion was waiting outside.

She rode up beside it and dismounted quickly without waiting for a groom to come to her horse's head.

Then she ran up the steps and into the hall.

There were two footmen on duty, and she asked breathlessly:

"Where . . . is His . . . Grace?"

"He ain't come down yet, Miss," a footman replied, pointing with his finger up to the ceiling.

Before he had finished his sentence, Zoe was halfway up the stairs.

She reached the corridor of the State Rooms where her own room was.

The Master Suite was at the end of it.

She tore along, lifting her riding-skirts so that it should not hamper her.

She had almost reached the Master Suite, when the door opened and Hubert came out.

Zoe swept by him without speaking and into the Duke's bedroom.

He was ready for riding and just putting a finishing touch with his ivory-backed brushes to the hair on either side of his forehead.

As Zoe entered, he looked round in surprise.

She flung herself against him, crying as she did so:

"Save . . . me . . . save . . . me! They have . . . come for . . . me . . . I must . . . hide . . . Oh, please . . . hide me. I would . . . die rather than . . . go . . . back with . . . them."

The Duke laid down his brushes and put his arms around her.

"Now, what is all this?" he asked.

"They have . . . found me . . . Oh, hide . . . me . . . quickly . . . they will be . . . here at . . . any moment."

"Who are they?" the Duke enquired.

"Russians," Zoe said, "and I . . . recognised . . . Count Leo Purshlin . . . who is . . . with . . . them."

Her voice was almost incoherent with breathlessness and fear.

The Duke acted instantly without asking more questions.

He drew her quickly along the corridor to a Boudoir which connected with her own bedroom.

"Go inside," he said quietly, "and do not open the door until I come back to you."

"You . . . will . . . hide . . . me?" Zoe asked.

There was a desperate note in her voice.

"No-one will take you away from me," the Duke said firmly.

He pushed her into the room and shut the door.

Then, as he hurried along the corridor, he saw Hubert coming back towards him.

"Get the two revolvers out of the drawer of my Dressing-Table," he said sharply.

Hubert, after his training with him in India, did not ask questions.

He merely ran to obey in order.

The Duke was already halfway down the stairs to find there were three footmen in the hall.

He said to the one who was nearest:

"Send the horses back to the stables and be quick about it. Then come back here."

As the footman ran outside to do as he was told, the Duke said to the other two who were staring at him:

"Get Dawson and the other footman as quickly as possible. Hurry! Hurry!"

They ran off and only a few seconds later Dawson and the footman who had fetched him came into the hall.

He stood beside the Duke and waited until the

other two footmen and the one who had been sent to the horses appeared.

"Shut the door," the Duke ordered.

Then, as the men looked at him a little apprehensively, he said:

"Now, listen. In a few minutes four men who are Russians will arrive in a Chaise. When you open the door to them, they will see you, Dawson, and behind you at attention, you four footmen."

They were all listening intently, and the Duke went on:

"The man in charge of the Russians, Count Purshlin, will ask for Miss Zoe. You will reply: 'I regret, Sir, Miss Zoe and His Grace left half-an-hour ago. They are staying away for the night and will not be back here until tomorrow at noon.'"

The Duke's eyes were on Dawson to be sure he understood.

Then he continued:

"The Count may then ask you where Miss Zoe and I have gone."

"I should think he'd do that, Your Grace," Dawson agreed.

"Then you say," the Duke ordered, " 'His Grace said before he left he would deal on his return with any problems that arose and any visitors. I think that means His Grace does not wish to be disturbed.'"

The Duke paused again before he said:

"Is that clear?"

"Very clear, Your Grace," Dawson replied.

"Good," the Duke said, "and we hope he will withdraw until tomorrow. If, however, he insists on entering the house and searching for Miss Zoe, then Hubert, who will be standing at the top of the stairs, will shoot him."

One of the footmen gave an audible gasp.

The Duke, looking up to the top of the stairway where Hubert was standing, said:

"Do not kill him, Hubert. Shoot him either in the arm or the shoulder. Understand?"

"Of course, Your Grace," Hubert replied.

"That is all," the Duke said, looking at Dawson. "I trust you to carry out my instructions, and when the Russians leave, make certain that they are not creeping round the house or hiding in the Garden."

He started to walk up the stairs as he spoke.

He knew from the light in the footmen's eyes and the satisfaction in Dawson's that he had given them orders to which they responded eagerly.

There was excitement too on Hubert's face.

The Duke was aware that there was nothing his Valet enjoyed more than being in what he called "a tight corner."

As the Duke reached the top of the stairs, Hubert handed him the special revolver he had always carried in India.

The other, which was not unlike it, was in his left hand.

"Are they loaded?" the Duke asked.

"Of course, Your Grace," Hubert said, somewhat offended at the suggestion that he might not have got the revolvers ready for action.

The Duke did not say any more but went swiftly to the door into the Boudoir.

He knocked twice before he turned the handle.

When he entered the room, he thought for a moment it was empty.

Then Zoe rose from behind the sofa, where she had obviously been hiding.

She had taken off her riding-coat.

126

Her golden hair seemed to gleam in the room as if it were a star.

She ran towards the Duke, crying as she did so:

"What . . . have . . . you done? Where . . . can I . . . go? Would I be . . . safer in the . . . cellars?"

"You are perfectly safe here," the Duke said quietly.

Zoe had reached him, and now her hands were pressed against him.

She was looking up at him with terror in her eyes.

"They will . . . force their . . . way into . . . the house and . . . find me," she whispered. "Oh, please . . . understand I must . . . be hidden . . . somewhere they . . . will never . . . look . . . otherwise I must . . . die."

Her voice broke on the last word.

The Duke pulled her close against him.

"I will not let you die, my Darling," he said, and his lips were on hers.

For a moment Zoe did not realise what was happening.

Then, as the Duke held her closer and closer, his kiss became more possessive, more demanding.

She felt as if she melted into him and was no longer herself but part of him.

She had never been kissed.

But she knew this was as a kiss should be.

She felt a rapture moving up in her breasts which she had never known before.

The Duke kissed her for what seemed a long time before he raised his head.

Then he said:

"Do you really think I would let anyone, Russian or no Russian, take you from me? You are mine, my Darling!"

"It . . . cannot be . . . true," Zoe said hesitatingly.

As the Duke looked down at her he saw the fear had almost gone from her eyes.

There was a radiance on her face which made her a thousand times more beautiful even than before.

Then, as if she suddenly came back to reality, she said:

"What are . . . you saying . . . to me?"

"I am telling you that I love you," the Duke said. "I think, my Darling, that you love me a little."

"I did not . . . know it was . . . love until you . . . kissed me," Zoe whispered. "But now . . . I love . . . you, I . . . love . . . you."

Even as she spoke, her expression changed.

"Will they . . . take me . . . away? How can . . . you stop . . . them?" she cried.

"You are mine," the Duke said, "and no-one can take you from me."

"But you . . . do not . . . understand," Zoe insisted.

"There is a great deal I do not understand," the Duke said, "but first I want to know, having said you hate men, what you feel about me."

"I love . . . you," Zoe said, "you . . . know I do . . . I . . . love . . . you."

"Because you do not think of me as a man?" the Duke said with a slight smile. "But I am one."

"A very . . . wonderful and . . . very clever . . . man," Zoe said in a voice he could hardly hear. "But if the Count . . . knows I am . . . here he will . . . insist on my . . . going back to . . . Russia."

"You are quite safe," the Duke said, "because Dawson will tell him that you and I left here early this morning and will not be back until noon tomorrow."

"And you . . . think the Count . . . will believe . . . him?"

"He will," the Duke replied.

He sat down as he spoke and drew Zoe close to him.

He could feel through her thin muslin blouse that she was trembling.

"Do not be afraid. When I know exactly what is wrong, I shall be able to protect you."

"When I tell . . . you what is . . . wrong," Zoe stammered, "you . . . will understand why . . . you have . . . to hide me."

She gave a shiver.

"Are you quite certain . . . they will believe . . . Dawson and . . . go . . . away?"

"I think they will have no alternative," the Duke said, "and tomorrow, when they come back, I shall be able to prove to them that you have no intention of going back to Russia."

"I doubt if . . . they will . . . listen to you," Zoe said, "and . . . my Father is . . . very powerful."

The Duke settled himself more comfortably against the soft cushions on the sofa.

With his arm around Zoe, he made it easier for her to put her head on his shoulder.

"Now," he said, "tell me why you pretended to be concussed by the eruption of Mount Ararat."

"It was the . . . only way I . . . could . . . escape," Zoe said in a very small voice.

"From whom?" the Duke asked.

"From Prince Kaknovski," she murmured.

The Duke stared at her in sheer astonishment.

"Prince Kaknovski?" he echoed. "Why should you be running away from him? What had he to do with you in the first place?"

"He is wicked . . . bad . . . evil!" Zoe murmured, "and I . . . hate him. I knew . . . I would rather . . . die than . . . marry him."

129

"Marry him?" the Duke repeated, and now there was an incredulous note in his voice.

Zoe shut her eyes and put her head against the Duke's shoulder.

"My Father," she said in a very small voice, "is the ... Grand Duke Alexis."

The Duke was astonished.

This was certainly something he had not expected.

"Your Father wanted you to—marry Prince Kaknovski?" he asked.

"He is so very ... rich, and when he saw ... me I think he ... offered Papa a great deal of ... money if I became ... his wife."

The Duke did not speak, and Zoe went on:

"When Papa took me to ... his Palace and I realised how ... evil he was ... I knew I had to ... save myself."

"Of course you did," the Duke said gently, "it was very brave of you. Tell me what you did."

"I took one of my maid's ... dresses when she was ... downstairs having her ... meal and I slipped out of the Palace ... at night. I hurried ... away towards ... the Turkish border."

She paused and then continued:

"I knew where it was ... because ... Count Purshlin, who is here today ... had taken ... Papa and me for a ... drive to show us where the ... Prince's land ... ended and the Turkish ... began."

"That was very courageous and sensible of you," the Duke said. "So you escaped from the Palace."

"I escaped into Turkey," Zoe continued. "Just ... as I reached ... Dogubovazit, Mount Ararat erupted. There was a terrible ... commotion. Everyone was ... tearing about in a ... frantic state, and that enabled

me to . . . steal some food . . . without being . . . noticed."

The Duke tightened his arms as if he could not bear
to think of her being hungry.

He did not interrupt, and after a little while she
went on:

"When morning came . . . the eruption was . . . over
and I saw people going off to collect . . . the dead and
the wounded from the mountain. It was then I had
a sudden idea. I walked with them for a little while
and then, when I had an . . . opportunity I slipped . . .
away and threw myself down on . . . a place that was
free of the lava."

She paused for breath and then said more slowly:

"I was there for only about half-an-hour before
they . . . picked me up and . . . took me down to where
a number of people had . . . congregated, including
Mrs. Winstead and . . . the orphans."

"So you attached yourself to them," the Duke said.

"She had two small girls crying at the same time,"
Zoe said. "While she nursed one, I nursed the other,
and so I . . . managed to escape."

"I think it was very clever of you," the Duke said.
"Only someone very quick-witted could have thought
up a plan so unusual and so effective."

"It was effective because you had told them you
would arrange for them to be taken to England."

"If I had seen you, I would have been even keener
on having the orphans," the Duke said.

"You had just left, when the Greek who gave me
my name and another man brought me down from
the mountain. I think if Mrs. Winstead had not been
so excited at the thought of going to England, she
might have . . . sent me away. But when she found I
was . . . useful she said I could go . . . with them."

"We must be very grateful to her for making a decision which would make us both so happy," the Duke said gently.

Zoe stared up at him.

Then she said:

"You have forgotten that Count Purshlin will come back tomorrow. He will insist, because he is very frightened of my Father, on taking me . . . away . . . or, if I am not here, he will go on . . . searching until . . . he finds . . . me."

She gave a little sigh before she said:

"He must have been . . . searching for a . . . long time already, and Papa . . . never gives up . . . once he has set his mind . . . on something."

"In other words, he is determined you will marry Prince Kaknovski," the Duke said.

"Papa wants the money he has . . . offered him. He also was much impressed with the . . . Prince's Palace and his . . . luxurious standard of living."

The Duke thought of all the exotic indulgencies and the perversions on which he knew the Prince spent his money.

Anyone as young and innocent as Zoe would be appalled at what went on in the Palace at night, and, for that matter, in the daytime.

Because he hated the idea of Zoe coming into contact with anything so revolting, the Duke said sharply:

"Just forget them! I promise you, my Darling, you will never come in contact with Prince Kaknovski again. So we will not even think about him."

"I knew . . . when I . . . saw him," Zoe said, "he was like some . . . evil monster and the . . . expression in his eyes . . . frightened me. When he . . . touched my . . . hand I . . . wanted to . . . scream."

The Duke knew it was her Russian blood that made her feel like that.

The Russians were very sensitive.

Although they had been his enemies in the *Great Game*, he had in fact several Russian friends who were very different.

Their feelings were deeply intensive rather than just on the surface.

To a Russian, his soul was the most important part of his body.

When he loved with his soul, it was a love that could never die because it was part of eternity.

As the Duke looked down at Zoe, he could see the love she felt for him shining in her eyes.

He knew it came from her soul.

He could understand now only too well why she had hated men.

He swore to himself he would be the last.

"Now, listen, my Precious," he said. "Now you have told me what has frightened you, you have to take only one step more to make quite certain that you are safe for ever."

"What . . . do I have . . . to do?" Zoe asked.

He felt the little tremour that ran through her and knew that once again she was afraid.

"It is quite simple," the Duke said very quietly. "You just have to answer one question."

"Question?" Zoe queried. "What is it?"

For a moment the Duke paused as if he were feeling for words.

Then he said:

"I am asking you, my Darling, if you will do me the great honour of becoming my wife."

For a moment it seemed as if Zoe gleamed with a light that was more brilliant than that of the sun.

Then, as if she felt she could not have heard him aright, she stammered:

"But . . . y-you . . . said you . . . w-would never . . . m-marry."

"That was before I met you," the Duke said, "and you said you hated all men."

She moved a little nearer to him.

"I also said, if you remember, that I did not think of you as . . . a man. If you can . . . save me, I will worship . . . you as a . . . God and . . . love you with all my heart."

The Duke kissed her until Zoe felt as if the sun had been caught in her breast.

The glory of it encompassed them both.

Then he put her very gently away from him and rose to his feet.

"What are you going to do?" she asked.

"I am going to find out if the Count has come and left, which I am quite sure he has," he replied. "There has been no sound of a shot, so I assume he is still unscathed. Then I am going to arrange that when he returns tomorrow, there will be no question of your returning to Russia to your Father."

Zoe looked bewildered, and he said:

"By then you will be my wife, my Precious, and by the law of this country, or any other for that matter, no-one can take a man's wife away from him once she bears his name."

Zoe gave a little cry of happiness, and the Duke said:

"Just to make certain that your Russians are not watching the house and creeping round trying to find out if you are here, we shall spend the rest of the day up here. So put on something comfortable, my Lovely One, and I will be as quick as I can."

The Duke kissed her again gently but possessively.

Then he forced himself to leave her and hurried to the door.

As soon as he was outside, he realised Hubert was nowhere to be seen.

This meant the Russians had come and gone.

Dawson was, however, waiting for him in the hall.

When he reached him, the butler said:

"The Russians arrived just as Your Grace said they would. The Count, who you said was in charge, obviously considered for some seconds forcing his way into the house to look for Miss Zoe. However, we were six to his four and he turns round disgusted like and drives away."

"Did you watch until they reached the end of the drive?" the Duke asked.

"Yes, Your Grace," Dawson replied. "He was a'travelling quite fast. I thinks, if I'm not mistaken, they had come here by sea."

"By sea?" the Duke repeated.

"Yes, Your Grace. There was something about two of the men as makes me think they be Seamen."

The Duke thought this was possible.

His home was only two miles from the sea.

If they had intended to take Zoe away in a hurry and were not expecting serious opposition, the easiest way would be to have a fast steam-yacht cruising off the coast.

The Duke, however, did not say any more to Dawson but went to his Secretary's room.

Mr. Bennett had been his Father's Secretary, and was more knowledgeable about the house and the Estate than anyone else.

He was also extremely intelligent.

When the Duke told him what he wished to do, he was controlled enough to show little surprise except when he heard who Zoe's Father was.

"I thought, Your Grace," he said, "that Miss Zoe was not entirely English. But it did not occur to me that she might come from the Royal Family of Russia."

"It makes things a little more difficult," the Duke said, "and therefore, Bennett, we have to be very careful in everything we do."

"I understand, Your Grace," Mr. Bennett said. "I will leave at once for Canterbury. It should take me, as Your Grace knows, about two hours each way."

The Duke nodded.

He then went to his Study and wrote a letter to the Marquis of Heatherdown, who was the Lord Lieutenant of Kent.

Then, having sent the letter off by a groom, he went to find his Grandmother.

It was still too early for her to have come downstairs.

But she looked very beautiful in one of the magnificently draped State beds.

"How nice to see you, Ivor," she said. "I suppose you have been riding."

"Not this morning, Grandmama," the Duke said, "owing to an extraordinary occurrence which has forced me to take immediate action on which I need your help."

The Dowager Duchess looked up at him a little apprehensively as he sat down beside the bed.

In a few short sentences he told her who Zoe was, and that her Father was determined to marry her to the most debauched and unpleasant man in the whole of Russia.

The Dowager listened very carefully to everything her grandson was saying.

When he told her that he and Zoe were going to be

married at once, she gave a little cry of delight.

"That is what I want to hear, dear boy," she said. "I have already found Zoe, as I shall continue to call her, charming and exactly the sort of wife I would want for you."

"Do you really mean that, Grandmama?" the Duke said.

"You know I would not lie to you over anything so important as your marriage," the Dowager said. "And if you had consulted me, which you did not, I would have told you I did not particularly care for Lady Lois Minford."

She looked at her grandson and went on:

"I did not trust all those shy looks and blushes. Appearing occasionally they are an expression of innocence, but when they are performed so often, they seem to be too much like a scene from Drury Lane."

The Duke threw back his head and laughed.

"Grandmama, you are wonderful!" he said. "I am sure no-one could deceive you for long,"

"I hope not," the Dowager said, "because if I have learned nothing else in life, I have learned the difference between the good grain and the chaff."

The Duke laughed again.

He thought as he did so that his Grandmother was much more astute than most people realised.

He did not speak of Lois again.

The Dowager went on to say how impressed she was with the way Zoe had behaved in what must have been very difficult circumstances.

"To pretend to have lost one's memory," she said, "day after day, week after week, must have been an excessively demanding task."

The Duke could not help remembering that at times

Zoe had given him a clue such as when he spoke of his private theatre.

He knew now that she had probably been thinking of the theatre Catherine the Great had added to the Winter Palace at St. Petersburg.

Or the Grand Duke himself might have one, as many of the Russian nobility had.

Aloud he said:

"I now have to get in touch with my private Chaplain and of course see to the decoration of the Chapel."

He put his hand on the Dowager Duchess's arm and asked:

"Would you, please, Grandmama, see what Mrs. Partridge has in her magic cupboards to make Zoe look like a Bride?"

He paused for a moment before he added:

"I want us to remember our wedding-day as something vastly important in both our lives."

There was a smile on the Dowager Duchess's lips and a faint suspicion of a tear in her eyes as he left the room.

She had worried more than she had let anyone know over her beloved grandson.

She knew how he had been pursued by women ever since he had grown up.

She had known that most of them, beautiful though they were, were not worthy of him.

She was afraid that he would be disappointed in his marriage, that he would be quickly bored with any young girl who became his wife.

He himself was so intelligent, so clever.

There were few men and certainly no women who could keep up with him when it came to a war of words, or, for that matter, a duel of hearts.

But now the Dowager Duchess thought nothing could be better than that he should marry a Russian.

She remembered the Grand Duke Alexis had married a friend of hers who had been a *débutante* with her.

Looking back, she could remember quite clearly that the Duke of Huntingfordshire's daughter had golden hair the same as Zoe's.

She had made a brilliant marriage at the end of her first Season by marrying into the Russian Royal Family.

The best of England and the best of Russia.

What could be a better combination to make what she hoped and prayed would be the perfect wife for Ivor?

She felt as if the sunshine coming through the window not only illuminated the room, but was part of her heart because she was so happy.

Zoe was taking off her riding-habit, when Mrs. Partridge came into the room.

"I have just been told the wonderful news by Her Grace," she said.

Zoe looked at her in surprise, and Mrs. Partridge went on:

"I am to find you a wedding-dress, Miss Zoe, and, believe it or not, I have two or three from which you can choose."

Zoe gave a little laugh.

"Your Aladdin's cave never fails, Mrs. Partridge," she said. "But I hope no-one else in the house knows what is happening."

She was suddenly afraid that the servants might talk.

If it somehow reached the village, the Russians sent by her Father might hear of it and force their way into the house.

They would seize her away before she could become the Duke's wife.

"You are quite safe, Miss," Mrs. Partridge said quickly. "When Her Grace told me, she informed me at the same time that no-one else is to know what has happened until after your marriage has taken place tonight."

"Then please, please, Mrs. Partridge," Zoe said, "make me look as pretty as you can for His Grace. It would be terrible if he were disappointed."

"He'll not be that, I promise you," Mrs. Partridge said. "Now, before you put on a dress, let me show you what I have hidden away."

* * *

Because the Duke knew it would make Zoe feel safer, they had dinner in her Boudoir.

By this time he had managed very cleverly without upsetting anyone that his guests had all departed.

The only exceptions were Charles, his Grandmother, and her daughter and son-in-law, the Earl and Countess of Evesham.

The Duke had particularly wanted the Earl to stay because he was the Secretary of State for India.

He had also invited the Lord Lieutenant, the Marquess of Heatherdown.

When dinner was finished, and it had been a very pleasant one, Zoe retired to her bedroom.

The Countess of Evesham said she had a headache and hoped the Duke would forgive her if she went to bed.

"The truth is," she said, "I am getting old and find these late nights too much for me."

"Grandmama is really much younger than any of us," the Duke said.

"I wish that were true," the Dowager Duchess said, laughing. "But I would have to be very old indeed to miss the wedding of my beloved grandson."

She looked affectionately at the Duke as she spoke.

He was, however, glancing down at his watch and then at the clock on the mantelpiece.

He was wondering what could have happened to Mr. Bennett.

He had left in good time to get the Special Licence at Canterbury.

He should have been back, allowing for every possible delay, at least two hours ago.

The Duke knew that his private Chaplain would already be downstairs in the Chapel.

He was anxious that something had gone wrong when the door opened and Dawson announced:

"The Archbishop of Canterbury, Your Grace."

The Duke looked up in astonishment as the Archbishop came into the room.

Then, as the Duke went towards him, he said:

"How could you imagine, Ivor, that I would allow you to get married in this hurry without me?"

"I did not dare to ask you," the Duke said.

"I baptised and confirmed you, and now I insist on joining you in holy matrimony," the Archbishop said.

The Dowager Duchess held out both her hands.

"It is the best thing I have ever heard," she said, "I am so very, very pleased that you have come."

"And I am delighted to see you again," the Archbishop answered. "Do not tell me the Bride is more beautiful than you, because I do not believe it."

They were all laughing.

The Duke thought that nothing could be more perfect than that he should have his marriage exactly as he wanted it.

He had always dreaded the idea of several hundred people crowded into St. George's, Hanover Square, or having to listen to tiresome speeches and shake hands hundreds of times on a hot summer's day.

Now he was going to be married in his own Chapel in his own house to a woman he truly loved, with only a few people present who really cared for him.

He knew now that what he had felt for Lois had just been a yearning for romance.

What he felt for Zoe, what in fact he had felt ever since he met her, was far stronger, far deeper and far more wonderful.

His marriage would take place in ten minutes' time, and he was the luckiest man in the whole world.

chapter seven

THE Archbishop accompanied by the Dowager Duchess, the Lord Lieutenant, and the Earl went down to the Chapel.

The Duke went first to his bedroom.

There he added to his evening-clothes his various decorations and the Order of the Garter.

Then he went to Zoe's bedroom, where he knew she would be waiting for him.

She was ready and looking so lovely that for a moment he could only stare at her and wonder if she was real.

She looked very different from her appearance, as he had arranged it, at the family Dinner at which he had saved himself from having to marry Lois.

Mrs. Partridge had produced no less than three wedding-gowns.

One had been worn by the Duke's Mother, another by his Grandmother, and the third by the Duchess who had been married in the days of Queen Anne.

Zoe had looked at them all, then chosen the one which had been worn by the Duke's Mother.

When she put it on, it became her more than any other gown could have done.

His mother had been married soon after Queen Victoria had introduced the bertha to London.

This particular one was embroidered with pearls and diamonds.

The top of Zoe's shoulders were bare.

The gown itself had a very small waist and a full skirt.

It made her look very young.

Although it was not a plain and simple white like that in which she had appeared as a Greek goddess, she looked innocent and untouched, just as the Duke would want her to be.

The train which the Duke's Mother had worn was too heavy for Zoe to manipulate without pages.

But Mrs. Partridge produced a wedding-veil of so fine a fabric that it might have been woven by a spider rather than by human hands.

It fell over the back of her gown and onto the floor, making a natural train behind her.

It was when she was looking at herself in the mirror that Mrs. Partridge brought in the family jewels.

"I think this is the tiara, Miss Zoe, His Grace would want you to wear," Mrs. Partridge said, "because it was his Mother's favourite. Whenever she was wearing it she always came to say good night to him so that he could admire it."

Zoe thought it was very beautiful.

Shaped like a crown, it had diamonds all round it in the form of stars which might have fallen from the sky.

There were also tiny diamond stars to wear in her

ears and a necklace to match.

When Zoe saw herself in the mirror she could hardly believe that she was not a fairy-tale figure rather than a human Bride.

Mrs. Partridge added a bracelet around each of her wrists, and then she said:

"His Grace told me to leave you when you are ready and he himself will take you down to the Chapel."

Zoe was sure that this was because the Duke knew she would want his protection.

She thanked Mrs. Partridge for all she had done and sat down on the stool in front of the dressing-table.

Even now she could hardly believe that she would become the Duke's wife without her Father's men interfering.

They might still spirit her away at the last moment.

She felt sure the Duke had taken every precaution.

At the same time, she knew the Russians better than he did.

When they were determined, they would never give up, however impossible their objective might seem.

She waited for nearly ten minutes.

She knew, because there was no sound from the Boudoir, that the others had gone to the Chapel.

She could not understand why the Duke did not come to her.

"Has something," she asked herself, "gone wrong at the last moment? Has the Duke tried to send the Russians away and have they wounded or killed him?"

Because she was so frightened, she sprang to her feet.

Even as she did so, the door opened and the Duke came in.

Without thinking, Zoe ran towards him, saying:

"Are you all right? You have . . . not been . . . hurt? Are . . . the Russians . . . here?"

The Duke put his arms around her.

"I am all right, my Darling. The delay is nothing to do with the Russians, but simply because the Archbishop of Canterbury has come himself to marry us."

"The Archbishop!" Zoe excalimed.

"He said that as he had baptised and confirmed me, he could not allow anyone else to marry me," the Duke explained. "So, my Precious, I will now take you down to the Chapel and I promise you need not be afraid."

"Forgive . . . me . . . I should have . . . trusted you," Zoe murmured.

She spoke humbly, and the Duke thought how lovely she looked as she did so.

But for the moment he could not find words to tell her how much he loved her.

Instead, he raised her hand to his lips and kissed it.

Then he offered her his arm and they moved out of the bedroom and into the corridor.

Outside, lying on a table, was the bouquet he had chosen for her.

She was not surprised that it was of white Orchids with just a few small lilies.

They moved slowly down side by side.

As they did so, the Duke was thinking that he had taken every possible precaution to make sure that nothing should interrupt the sanctity and beauty of their wedding.

There were four game-keepers with their shotguns

on guard outside the Chapel.

Inside, at the back where they could hardly be seen, were Hubert and two footmen, all armed.

The Duke had put Charles in charge of security around the whole house.

He was now waiting in the Chapel to act as the Duke's best man.

As Zoe came in through the door, one glance at the Chapel itself told her that the Duke, to express his love, had given her the most valuable present in his possession.

The whole of the altar and the chancel was decorated with the Orchids from his special greenhouse.

They were there blooming in their brilliant colours, fragile and exquisite in the light from the candles in their golden candlesticks.

The Archbishop of Canterbury was standing waiting for them as they moved up the aisle.

The Duke's private Chaplain was in attendance.

The Archbishop recited the order of service with a sincerity which made Zoe feel as if every word he spoke blessed them.

She was sure no woman could have a more wonderful wedding.

When the Duke put the ring on her finger she knew that he was as moved as she was by the service.

When they knelt for the Blessing she felt as if a brilliant light enveloped them both which came from Heaven.

When the service was over, they went from the Chapel into the Drawing-Room.

The chandeliers were lit.

The whole great house, which had appeared to be unoccupied during the day in case the Russians were watching it, was now ablaze with light.

They stayed only a short time with their guests in the Drawing-Room because the Archbishop had to return to Canterbury.

The Duke begged him to stay the night but he said he had an early Communion.

When the Duke and Zoe thanked him for marrying them, he said:

"It has given me the greatest pleasure. I have always prayed that Ivor would find the real love that we all seek, and I know now it is his."

As soon as he had gone, the Duke and Zoe said good-night to the others, and he led her upstairs.

When they reached her room, to her surprise he did not stop but walked on towards the Master Suite.

She did not ask questions, but when he opened the door she understood.

The huge bedroom in which the Dukes of Stalbridge had slept for generations was a bower of flowers.

They were all white, mostly lilies and roses, and their fragrance filled the air.

There was one exception: the *Chusua Donii* Orchid from Tibet had been placed in front of the window as if it were a shrine.

"How could you have done . . . this so . . . quickly," Zoe asked, "and for . . . me?"

"For my wife," the Duke said, "whom I will love for as long as we both live."

He stood looking at her for a moment, and then he said:

"I thought tonight neither of us would want to talk to Servants. Can you manage to undress yourself, or shall I help you?"

"I can . . . manage," Zoe said shyly.

The Duke did not say anything and went out by

another door in the side wall of the room.

Because she knew he expected it of her, Zoe undressed quickly.

There was a pretty nightgown lying on the bed, waiting for her.

She put it on and slipped into bed.

Now she could see under the great carved canopy overhead that the Duke had not had the curtains pulled.

She could see the stars in the sky.

None of it somehow seemed real—the profusion of flowers, the Orchid, and the moon sending a silver beam through the window.

"I . . . am dreaming . . . I must be . . . dreaming," Zoe said. to herself.

Then the Duke came in.

He sat down on the side of the bed and took her hand in his.

"What are you thinking?" he asked.

"I am . . . sure I am . . . dreaming," Zoe said. "It is so . . . beautiful it . . . cannot be real."

"And you are no longer afraid?" the Duke asked.

There was silence.

Then he said gently:

"Tell me."

"I am not really . . . afraid of the . . . Russians now," Zoe began.

"But you are afraid of me?" the Duke asked quickly.

"Not of you," Zoe replied. "But you swore you would . . . never marry and now . . . suppose having . . . married me so . . . quickly you . . . find I am . . . disappointing, and you wish . . . you were . . . free?"

He knew by the way she spoke that the question was a very real one.

He took off the long robe he was wearing and threw it down on the chair.

Then he blew out the candles, got into bed, and took Zoe into his arms.

He felt her whole body quiver, not with fear but at his touch.

He said very gently:

"This is the only way, my Precious, that I can explain to you how much you mean to me and how different you are from anyone I have ever known before."

"Is that . . . really . . . true?" Zoe asked.

"Would I lie to you at this moment? I swear to you it is the truth and the whole truth that I have never until now been in love."

He gave a little sigh before he said:

"I have sought love, of course I have. What man does anything else? But I have always been disappointed and, before I met you, disillusioned."

"I thought . . . you must . . . have been . . . hurt," Zoe said.

"Because I was hurt, I decided I would not marry until I was old," the Duke said, "and then I met you and my whole world has changed."

"And you . . . love . . . me," Zoe whispered.

"I love you in a way I did not know existed," the Duke said, "and I know now, my Precious, we have both found something that is so wonderful, so perfect, and we must never lose it."

"I love . . . you," Zoe said, "because you are so . . . clever and because you are so . . . kind and . . . understanding."

"Are you quite sure you will never hate me?" the Duke asked.

She gave a little laugh because it sounded so absurd.

"I love . . . you, with . . . all of me and I know . . . there is no . . . end to my . . . love! It will . . . grow and . . . grow every . . . day and every . . . year that we are . . . together."

As she said the last words, she had a sudden fear.

Perhaps her Father, by some means of his own, would manage to separate them.

The Duke read her thoughts and pulled her close to him and said:

"You are mine and I will protect you, look after you, keep you safe. Nothing and no-one will ever separate us."

Zoe knew it was a vow, and then the Duke was kissing her, at first very gently, and then possessively, as if he were defying the world.

Zoe felt as if the stars had fallen down from the sky.

The flowers covered them both and the moonlight moved into their hearts.

It was an ecstasy and rapture which was different from anything she had ever known or imagined.

It carved them both into a magical world where there was no fear, only love.

Then, as the Duke made her his, they were swept into the sky, into a Heaven which exists only for lovers who are blessed by God Himself.

*   *   *

The following morning the Duke and Zoe had breakfast in the Sitting-Room adjacent to the Master Suite.

It was a long room which Zoe had never seen before and it too was full of flowers.

She was wearing only a *négligée* over her night-gown.

The Duke had on his long robe which gave him a Military appearance.

He had in fact worn it when he was in the Army.

Zoe poured her husband a second cup of coffee and then said in a low voice:

"What . . . have we . . . to do this . . . morning?"

"If I had my choice," the Duke said, "I would go back to bed and I would tell you again, my Darling, how much I love you."

There was a faint flush on Zoe's cheeks.

He thought it was like the dawn sweeping up in the sky and just as beautiful.

"I would . . . like that . . . too," she said in a shy little voice.

"Unfortunately," the Duke said, "we have one more official duty and then we are going on our Honeymoon."

Zoe's eyes opened wide.

"Honeymoon?"

"Of course," the Duke said. "I have planned something very exciting, my Darling, which I hope you will enjoy."

"Tell me about it," Zoe begged.

"We are going first," he said, "to a house I have near the sea which is not far from here. It is rather like an Italian villa and was built by my Grandfather because the Doctor said he must have fresh air and the sun."

"Is that what . . . we are going . . . to have?" Zoe asked.

"I also intend to teach you about love," the Duke said.

"That is . . . something I am . . . greatly looking . . . forward to," she replied.

Now there was no doubt that Zoe was blushing.

As if he could not prevent himself, he rose from the table and pulled her into his arms.

"How is it possible," he asked, "to make me feel like this."

"Like . . . what?" she questioned.

"As if I were floating in the clouds and at the same time galloping in silver armour to save you from every Dragon that ever existed."

Zoe laughed.

"I liked . . . that and I am . . . sure no Dragon would dare to . . . compete against . . . you."

Even as she spoke, she thought of the Russians and stiffened.

"Forget them!" the Duke said. "I assure you they will not come back."

"Are you quite . . . quite . . . certain of . . . that?" Zoe asked.

"Absolutely," he said.

She put her arms round his neck.

"I trust you, and I love you so much that I cannot say it in words."

The Duke picked her up in his arms.

"Why should we worry about words," he asked, "when there is a much better way to express what we feel for each other?"

He carried her back into the bedroom.

* * *

It was two hours later when Zoe rang for Mrs. Partridge and the Duke for Hubert.

When they went downstairs, Zoe found to her surprise that they were in a room she had never seen before.

"It was built by my Grandfather," the Duke explained. "Because he was a Statesman he was continually holding meetings and conferences, and needed a special room for them. When I was young I used to tease him and call it 'The Throne Room.' "

It was certainly, Zoe thought, very like one.

It was a large room built out on the East Wing.

It could easily seat two or three hundred people.

At the far end was a slightly raised dais with two high-backed chairs in the centre of it.

It made her think the Duke's name for it was very appropriate.

When she and the Duke entered the room, Zoe realised that he had thought out every detail.

He took her to the two chairs with the high backs in the centre of the dais.

She then saw that sitting on other chairs on one side of them was the Lord Lieutenant, on the other side the Duke's Uncle, the Earl of Evesham, Secretary of State for India.

As Zoe sat down she saw that on each side of the long room there were large windows, and lined up near the door she could see soldiers in uniform.

As if the Duke knew she was waiting for an explanation, he said:

"The Lord Lieutenant notified the Army camp at Chatham. They have sent us a detachment of the Brigade of Guards in charge of Major Montgomery."

'They certainly look,' Zoe thought, 'very resplendent in their red tunics and black bearskins.'

As well as the soldiers, there were two footmen on the door.

Even as Zoe and the Duke sat down on the dais there was a sound of marching feet in the distance.

Zoe looked quickly at the Duke for an explanation.

He was looking across the room.

The two footmen were standing with their hands on the large double doors at the entrance.

The marching feet came nearer and nearer.

Now, because she was frightened, Zoe clasped her fingers together so that they turned white.

The two footmen pulled the door open.

Standing in the entrance, Zoe could see Count Leo Purshlin.

Behind him were two of the men who had accompanied him yesterday.

Behind them were ten Seamen in Naval uniform.

She gave a little gasp.

Then she realised the footmen had allowed the Count to move into the Reception Room.

They had barred those accompanying him from coming any further than the doorway.

For a moment the Count seemed nonplussed.

Then he lifted his head high so he would not be intimidated.

He walked slowly and with dignity up the carpet which led him to the foot of the dais.

When he reached it he bowed to the Duke.

Then he said slowly in excellent English:

"On the orders of His Royal Highness, the Grand Duke Alexis of Russia, I have come to escort home Her Serene Highness Princess Natasha, who I understand is known to Your Grace as Miss Zoe."

His voice seemed to echo round the room.

There was dead silence before the Duke answered:

"I understand, Count, that you are carrying out orders you were given before you left St. Petersburg. Your mission is impossible, since Her Serene Highness Princess Natasha, who, as you say, has been known here as Miss Zoe, no longer exists."

The Count looked at the Duke in astonishment.

Then, before he could speak, the Duke continued in the quiet, grave tone in which he had spoken before:

"She is now in fact Her Grace the Duchess of Stalbridge, and my wife."

"I do not believe it," the Count said sharply.

"I thought," the Duke went on, ignoring what the Count had said, "that His Royal Highness would like to have a copy of our Marriage Certificate. The Princess and I were married by His Grace the Archbishop of Canterbury, and the witnesses were the Marquis of Heatherdown, Lord Lieutenant of Kent, who represented Her Majesty Queen Victoria, and the other witness was the Earl of Evesham, here on my left, who is Secretary of State for India."

As the Duke finished speaking he rose.

Picking up a large envelope from a small table beside his chair, he held it out to the Count.

Just for a moment the Russian hesitated before he took the envelope from the Duke.

At the same time, he knew he was defeated.

He glanced round as if he were considering whether to use violence or accept the inevitable.

There were twenty soldiers of the Brigade of Guards present besides the Officer in charge of them.

There were also the two footmen on the door who were still preventing his Seamen from entering the room.

With an effort the Count bowed and said:

"I will, Your Grace, convey this information to His Royal Highness."

"And will you tell His Royal Highness," the Duke added, "that my wife and I will be delighted if he would visit us here at Stalbridge Hall. When it is convenient, the Duchess and I will perhaps be able to visit His Royal Highness in St. Petersburg."

"I will tell His Royal Highness what Your Grace has said."

The Count glanced towards Zoe as if he thought she might have something to add.

She was, however, looking up at the Duke with admiring eyes.

After a moment the Count turned away.

It was quite an effort, the Duke knew, for him to walk back the way he had come to where his Seamen were waiting.

He was aware that he had failed in the mission with which he had been entrusted.

He had assumed it would be an easy victory for his Russian master.

Instead, he had to return empty-handed.

He knew that he would have to suffer under the Grand Duke's bad temper.

This was extremely unpleasant for its victims if he did not get his own way.

The Count passed through the doors at the end of the room.

Again there was the sound of marching feet as his Seamen followed him back the way they had come.

The Duke waited until there was silence.

Then with a sigh of relief he rose to his feet.

"I am glad that is over," he said.

Turning to the Major of the Grenadier Guards, he added:

"I am deeply grateful, Major, for your support. As you must realise, we should have been defenceless without it."

"I knew a large Russian steam-yacht was lying off Dover," the Major answered, "but I would not have believed the Russians would dare to abduct anyone from this country by force."

"Thanks to you," the Duke said, "it is something that has not happened. I hope, Major, you will allow your men to have a drink and celebrate our victory in the Servants' Hall. And you must join us for a glass of Champagne."

"I shall be delighted," the Major replied.

He gave an order to the Corporal, who marched the Grenadiers out of the Reception Room.

Without hurrying, the Duke and his guests walked towards the Drawing-Room.

The Dowager Duchess was waiting there for them.

When the Duke went forward to kiss her, she held out both her hands to Zoe.

"I have heard what has happened, my Dearest," she said, "and now there is nothing to frighten you, I understand that you and Ivor are going on your Honeymoon."

"That is what he has . . . just told . . . me," Zoe replied, "and it is very . . . exciting."

The Dowager Duchess smiled.

"I have never seen my Grandson look so happy," she said, "and that is what I have always wanted."

"He is so wonderful!" Zoe said.

The Dowager Duchess knew that her prayers were answered.

Her Grandson was being loved as she wanted him to be loved.

"I am to be very busy while you are away," she told Zoe.

"Why?" Zoe enquired.

"I have been instructed to start getting your trousseau," the Dowager answered. "As many gowns as possible will follow you to where you are staying first—the rest will catch up with you wherever you go."

Zoe gave a little cry of delight.

"Thank you! Thank you! I do want to look pretty for Ivor."

The Dowager Duchess smiled.

"You will, dear child," she said affectionately.

A moment later the Major left with his Grenadiers.

Zoe and the Duke had a quiet Luncheon with what was left of the House-Party.

Charles, who had been supervising everything for the Duke, now joined them.

Finally they were ready to leave in the Duke's special travelling Chaise with a team of four perfectly matched horses.

"I can only wish you what you wish for yourselves," Charles said. "I have never seen two people look so happy, and I have never been so sure that their happiness will last for ever."

"Thank you, Charles," the Duke said. "I want you to look after everything while we are away and see that the horses are properly exercised."

Charles laughed.

"You can be quite certain I will do that. When will you be back?"

"I have no idea," the Duke said. "We are going on a voyage of discovery to discover ourselves! We shall return only when we have so much to think about that we really need a rest."

Charles laughed again.

"Only you, Ivor, could think of anything like that."

The Duke started off his horses.

Zoe waved as they went down the drive.

Then she moved a little closer to the Duke so that she could put her hand on his knee.

"Are we ... really going ... away for so ... long?" she asked.

"For as long as you do not find me boring and want to step out of a dream world back into reality," the Duke replied.

"Then that . . . will be . . . for ever," Zoe said quickly.

"Of course there might be other reasons," the Duke suggested.

"Like . . . what?" Zoe asked.

"One is we might want our first child to be born at the Hall," the Duke replied.

Zoe turned her head and pressed it for a moment against his shoulder.

"I did . . . think of . . . that . . . myself," she whispered, "but I thought . . . you might be . . . shocked if I . . . said it."

"I will try not to shock you, my Lovely One," the Duke answered. "I have so many things to say to you that I have never said to anyone before but which are an indivisible part of our happiness."

Because he was speaking seriously, Zoe knew how much it meant to him.

Her Russian blood told her there was between them a bond which no-one could describe in words.

It was part of their souls, their minds, and the world in which they lived and breathed.

Last night when the Duke had made her his she had known she was the other half of him.

They were no longer two people but one.

Now she knew there was really no need for either of them to put their feelings into words.

Her heart was his heart, his soul was her soul.

They thought together, they breathed together.

It was all part of the miracle they had found together which was—Love.

ABOUT THE AUTHOR

Barbara Cartland, the world's most famous romantic novelist, who is also an historian, playwright, lecturer, political speaker and television personality, has now written 614 books and sold over six hundred and twenty million copies all over the world.

She has also had many historical works published and has written four autobiographies as well as the biographies of her mother and that of her brother, Ronald Cartland, who was the first Member of Parliament to be killed in the last war. This book has a preface by Sir Winston Churchill and has just been republished with an introduction by Sir Arthur Bryant.

Love at the Helm, a novel written with the help and inspiration of the late Earl Mountbatten of Burma, Great Uncle of His Royal Highness, The Prince of Wales, is being sold for the Mountbatten Memorial Trust.

She has broken the world record for the last twenty years by writing an average of twenty-three books a year. In the Guinness Book of World Records she is listed as the world's top-selling author.

Miss Cartland in 1987 sang an Album of Love Songs with the Royal Philharmonic Orchestra.

In private life Barbara Cartland, who is a Dame of the Order of St. John of Jerusalem and Chairman of the St. John Council in Hertfordshire, has fought for better conditions and salaries for Midwives and Nurses.

She championed the cause for the Elderly in 1956, invoking a Government Enquiry into the "Housing Condition of Old People."

In 1962 she had the Law of England changed so that Local Authorities had to provide camps for their own Gypsies. This has meant that since then thousands and thousands of Gypsy children have been able to go to School, which they had never been able to do in the past, as their caravans were moved every twenty-four hours by the Police.

There are now fifteen camps in Hertfordshire and Barbara Cartland has her own Romany Gypsy Camp called "Barbaraville" by the Gypsies.

Her designs "Decorating with Love" are being sold all over the U.S.A. and the National Home Fashions League made her, in 1981, "Woman of Achievement."

She is unique in that she was one and two in the Dalton list of Best Sellers, and one week had four books in the top twenty.

Barbara Cartland's book *Getting Older, Growing Younger* has been published in Great Britain and the U.S.A. and her fifth cookery book, *The Romance of Food*, is now being used by the House of Commons.

In 1984 she received at Kennedy Airport America's

Bishop Wright Air Industry Award for her contribution to the development of aviation. In 1931 she and two R.A.F. Officers thought of, and carried, the first aeroplane-towed glider airmail.

During the War she was Chief Lady Welfare Officer in Bedfordshire, looking after 20,000 Servicemen and women. She thought of having a pool of Wedding Dresses at the War Office so a Service Bride could hire a gown for the day.

She bought 1,000 gowns without coupons for the A.T.S., the W.A.A.F.'s and the W.R.E.N.S. In 1945 Barbara Cartland received the Certificate of Merit from Eastern Command.

In 1964 Barbara Cartland founded the National Association for Health of which she is the President, as a front for all the Health Stores and for any product made as alternative medicine.

This is now a £65 million turnover a year, with one-third going in export.

In January 1968 she received *La Médeille de Vermeil de la Ville de Paris*. This is the highest award to be given in France by the City of Paris. She has sold 30 million books in France.

In March 1988 Barbara Cartland was asked by the Indian Government to open their Health Resort outside Delhi. This is almost the largest Health Resort in the world.

Barbara Cartland was received with great enthusiasm by her fans, who feted her at a reception in the City, and she received the gift of an embossed plate from the Government.

Barbara Cartland was made a Dame of the Order of the British Empire in the 1991 New Year's Honours List by Her Majesty, The Queen, for her contribution to

Literature and also for her years of work for the community.

Dame Barbara has now written more than 614 books, the greatest number by a British author, passing the 564 books written by John Creasey.

AWARDS

1945   Received Certificate of Merit, Eastern Command, for being Welfare Officer to 5,000 troops in Bedfordshire.

1953   Made a Commander of the Order of St. John of Jerusalem. Invested by H.R.H. The Duke of Gloucester at Buckingham Palace.

1972   Invested as Dame of Grace of the Order of St. John in London by The Lord Prior, Lord Cacia.

1981   Received "Achiever of the Year" from the National Home Furnishing Association in Colorado Springs, U.S.A., for her designs for wallpaper and fabrics.

1984   Received Bishop Wright Air Industry Award at Kennedy Airport, for inventing the aeroplane-towed Glider.

1988   Received from Monsieur Chirac, The Prime Minister, The Gold Medal of the City of Paris, at the Hotel de la Ville, Paris, for selling 25 million books and giving a lot of employment.

1991   Invested as Dame of the Order of The British Empire, by H.M. The Queen at Buckingham Palace for her contribution to Literature.